THE FIFTH QUEEN

ALI HOUSE

Published in Canada by Engen Books, St. John's, NL.

Library and Archives Canada Cataloguing in Publication

Title: The fifth queen / Ali House.
Names: House, Ali, 1982- author.
Description: Series statement: The segment delta archives ; 2
Identifiers: Canadiana 2019005400X | ISBN 9781926903958 (softcover)
Classification: LCC PS8615.O867 F54 2019 | DDC C813/.6—dc23

Distributed by:
Engen Books
www.engenbooks.com
submissions@engenbooks.com

First mass market paperback printing: March 2019

Cover Image: Melody Pond
http://melodyypond.weebly.com/

THE FIFTH QUEEN

Erikson Family Tree

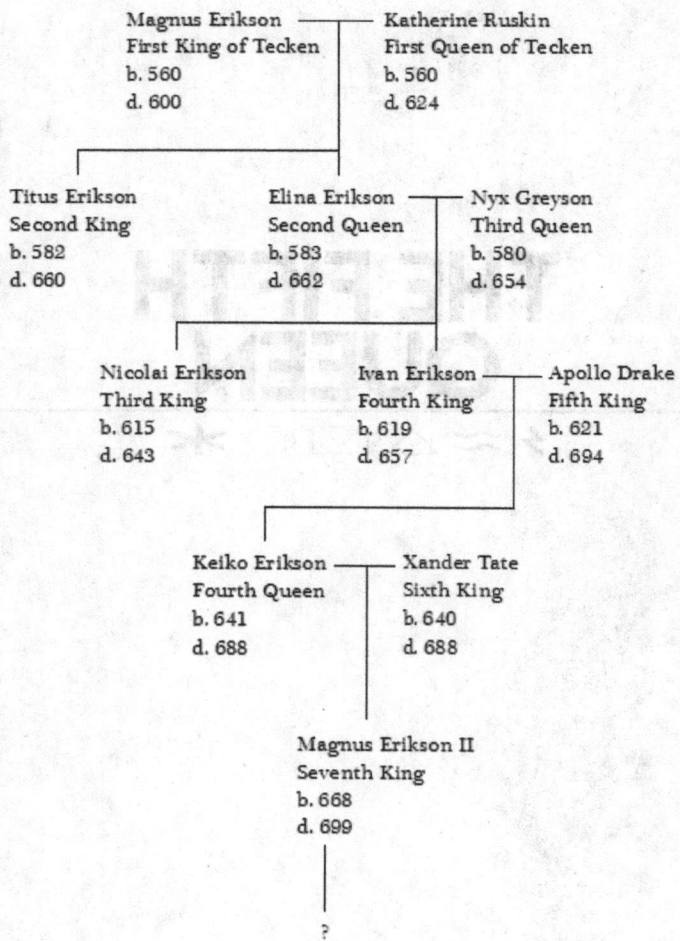

Magnus Erikson
First King of Tecken
b. 560
d. 600

Katherine Ruskin
First Queen of Tecken
b. 560
d. 624

Titus Erikson
Second King
b. 582
d. 660

Elina Erikson
Second Queen
b. 583
d. 662

Nyx Greyson
Third Queen
b. 580
d. 654

Nicolai Erikson
Third King
b. 615
d. 643

Ivan Erikson
Fourth King
b. 619
d. 657

Apollo Drake
Fifth King
b. 621
d. 694

Keiko Erikson
Fourth Queen
b. 641
d. 688

Xander Tate
Sixth King
b. 640
d. 688

Magnus Erikson II
Seventh King
b. 668
d. 699

?

$\lightning \approx \triangle \square \bigcirc *$

PART ONE

$\lightning \approx \triangle \square \bigcirc *$

CHAPTER 1
693 A.R. (AFTER REBUILDING)

The newborn's cries rang throughout the birthing room. While a nurse tended to the infant, a young woman lay on the bed, looking out the nearby window. Exhaustion coursed through her limbs and sweat plastered her bright red hair to her face, but she felt a sense of triumph now that the whole ordeal was over with. Instead of concentrating on breathing or pushing, all she needed to do was lie back and admire the beautiful sunset.

The woman had come to the hospital by herself and refused to contact any friends or family. The only phone call she allowed the receptionist to make was to an adoption agency, to say that the child was on the way. During the birth, a second nurse had come in to hold her hand and coach her along. This nurse had tried to make small talk by enquiring about the child's father, but the woman pretended that she hadn't heard the question and refused to answer. The nurse quickly realized that personal questions were not a welcome subject and refrained from asking any more, leaving the room as soon as her services were no longer required.

The child's cries quieted down, and the nurse asked the young woman if she would like to hold her, but she ignored his question, never taking her green eyes off the sky and the way it slowly darkened from pink to red. It was only when the adoption clerk walked into the room that she looked away, giving the clerk her full attention. Much of the important information had been sorted out beforehand, as privacy was very important to the woman, so there were only a few cursory questions left. The clerk went through his list and the woman answered quickly and efficiently, already eager for this to be over with.

Once they had finished, the nurse wheeled the newborn over, stopping near the bed as he asked the clerk a question. While they talked, the woman looked down at the sleeping child: her dark skin stood out against the pale, yellow blanket she had been wrapped in, and dark hair crowned her head. The woman couldn't help wondering if the child had the same eyes as her biological father. If she could choose, she would want this baby to have the same drive and determination. She wanted the world to open up its arms and give this child everything it could offer – and everything she could not. There was a part of her that wondered what it would've been like for the father to be here, holding her hand, smiling at their child. The young woman knew why it couldn't be that way, and although it hurt, she wouldn't have changed anything.

The nurse nodded at the clerk's instructions and wheeled the child out of the room. The clerk turned to follow, but the woman called out to him. She hadn't planned on making any requests but had suddenly been struck with a thought. Taking a deep breath for courage, she asked if she could suggest a name for the baby. The clerk nodded and readied his pen.

The woman glanced over at the sky, which had darkened to a deep purple, and spoke:

Kendra.

CHAPTER 2
6 YEARS LATER (699 A.R.)

"And *that* is why Tecken is the bestest island in the whole of Segment Delta!" Pitor Ruskin spread his arms wide, giving his story the big finish that was required by his audience.

The six-year-old girl sitting in front of him clapped her hands enthusiastically and a large smile broke out on her face. "Another, Unky Petey!"

"All right, Kendra," he smiled. "Any requests?"

"Umm..." Her head tilted to the side and her mouth fell open as she considered which story she most wanted to hear.

Pitor tried to hide how much this amused him. She took story time very seriously and would not have appreciated him laughing at her.

It was his job to entertain Kendra in the living room while her mothers and his husband talked in the dining room. As much as he would have liked to be involved in the conversation, he knew that it was important to keep Kendra distracted. Besides, his husband would fill him in later.

"How about the boy who played with fire?" he suggested helpfully.

"No... Heard that one a million billion times." She rocked from side to side as she tried to figure out which story she wanted to hear the most. "Can Unky Fizy tell me the story about the girl who planted rocks?"

Pitor put a hand to his heart and gasped in an exaggerated manner. "Are Unky Petey's stories not good enough anymore?"

"No, but Unky Fizy makes the ground shake, just like in the story."

"Ah, so you like Earth more than Fire?" he teased, snapping his fingers. His green eyes glowed red as a small flame appeared above his thumb. He let the flame flicker a few times, just long enough for a smile to cross Kendra's face, before blowing it out.

"I like *all* elements, Unky Petey."

"So, you won't be sad if you get dumb old Fire as your element when you turn twenty-one?" He put on an exaggerated frown.

She shook her head vehemently, her dark purple hair flying around her face. "Nope. What are Mama and Mommy talking to Unky Fizy about? They're all quiet and seer-ee-ous."

Pitor looked over at the dining room. The mood around the table was subdued, with heads close and voices low, unlike their usual talks, and it wasn't surprising that even a six-year-old could pick up on it. "It's nothing to worry yourself about," he reassured Kendra. "Have you picked another story yet?"

"Mommy was really quiet on the walk over," she said, ignoring him. She began to trace some whimsical design on the floor, her index finger gliding over the wood-grain in unidentifiable patterns. There was a sad look in her grey eyes. "Unky Petey, did I do something wrong?"

"Of course not!" Pitor sat next to her and put an arm around her shoulder. "They're talking about serious things, because something very important is going to happen soon."

"What is it?"

Pitor took in a deep breath. She was too young to understand exactly what was going on, but he had to tell her something. "You know how there are six islands in our Segment, and all of them are controlled by the Council of Twelve, except for us? How we're no longer connected to the other islands, and we follow Magnus Erikson and make our own rules?"

She nodded.

"Well, the Council doesn't like that. They see our freedom as a threat, and they want us back under their control. See, they're worried that if other people see how good life is over here, they'll want to break away and form their own governments, just like we did."

"But what's wrong with that?"

"Some people love having control over others and they'll do anything not to lose it. We don't want to join them, so they'll try to conquer us by force. Which is why we have to defend ourselves."

Kendra's face screwed up into a frown as she tried to understand. "Like when Byl hit Lila 'cause she took his blocks?"

"Kind of. It's a bit more serious than that."

"It's really seer-ee-ous?"

"*Really* serious. If we don't win this fight, then the other side is going to come over here and make us change everything, and we'll end up losing a lot of the things we like."

"Are Mama and Mommy going to fight?"

Pitor nodded. "They want to make sure you grow up in a good world."

Her lower lip stuck out. "But what if I don't want them to fight?"

"Nobody wants to fight, sweetie," he said. "But we have to if we want to protect ourselves and our neighbours. Luckily your mama and mommy will be here, on the island. They'll only have to fight if the bad people make it past all our soldiers and come over here, which I'm sure they won't."

"Oh." Kendra smiled brightly, but her smile fell away as fast as it had arrived. "But what about Unky Fizy? Is he staying here too?"

"Fizy..." Pitor's voice faltered. "Fizy also wants to make sure you grow up safe and sound, so he's going over with the other soldiers to stop the bad people from coming here."

"So, he's going to fight?"

He nodded.

She went back to tracing patterns on the floor. "But after the fighting is over, he'll tell me my story, right?"

As Pitor stared at the man he had spent the past ten years of his life with, uncertainty crossed his face. No matter how prepared they were, there was always a possibility of something going wrong – especially during a war.

He quickly shook off the feeling and smiled at Kendra. "Of course he will."

Δ

An hour later, Kendra and her mothers headed home. Pitor and Fitz smiled and waved goodbye, but as soon as the front door was closed, Pitor let out a heavy sigh.

"Rough visit?" Fitz said with a hint of amusement in his voice.

Pitor nodded. "She asked a lot of tough questions. I kept trying to change the subject, but she wouldn't be deterred."

"Well, if anyone knows how to put a spin on things, it's you." Fitz wrapped his arms around Pitor and laid his head on his shoulder.

Pitor closed his eyes and leaned into the hug, enjoying the peaceful moment. Talking strategy with adults was one thing, but explaining a war like this to a child was completely different. There were a lot of politics and reasoning that needed to be simplified, and each word had to be carefully chosen. It had been surprisingly exhausting.

Although Fitz and he had been married for nine years, they'd never desired children of their own. Still, they were delighted when their close family friends, Alix and Jaya Chen adopted Kendra. Although Pitor never turned down an opportunity to babysit, he often appreciated the quiet that came after Kendra's parents took her home.

"It won't be long now," Fitz said, breaking the silence. "Erikson's putting the final pieces into play, and then we'll march. It'll likely happen within the week."

"I'm surprised that he's doing this so soon," Pitor said. He walked over to the couch and sat down. This might end up being a long conversation and he wanted to be comfortable.

"Well," Fitz leaned against the fireplace mantel, "as the saying goes, strike while the iron's hot."

Pitor nodded, but he couldn't help feeling that Erikson was rushing into this war. The plan to invade Stanton and fight the ISS had always seemed inevitable, but during the past month the plan had gained enormous momentum. Fitz worked for the Tecken Army as a captain, so he knew more than most people, including information about Tecken's secret weapon. Pitor had his reservations about this weapon, wondering if it would work as well as everyone hoped. Although Pitor believed wholeheartedly in Erikson, he couldn't help wondering why he was choosing to fight now, instead of waiting the few months until the new year. Pitor had always had a suspicion that some kind of conflict would happen next year, as 700 A.R. would be exactly one hundred years after Magnus Erikson the First invaded Stanton and started the first war in New Earth's history. Despite being highly intelligent and analytical, Magnus Erikson the Second was also a man who believed in signs. He tried to emulate his great-grandfather and namesake in all matters, and Pitor often wondered if it was true that Erikson had never received an elemental vision, or if he'd had one and declined it in order to be just like his great-grandfather.

Despite what he'd told Kendra, there was no immediate threat from their enemies. In fact, he was certain that if a war was going to happen, they would have to initiate it, as The Council of Twelve was too scared to cause conflict. So why wasn't Erikson waiting?

"You're worried," Fitz said.

Pitor rolled his eyes. "Of course I am. War isn't a trifling matter." He looked over at his husband, whose short green hair always seemed to be perfectly in place, no matter what the situation. The white shirt he was wearing complimented his bronze skin and red eyes, but the smile that started to appear on Pitor's face quickly vanished as he felt the same uncertainty from his conversation with Kendra.

Fitz saw this change and walked over to the couch, sitting down next to him. "You know that I'm not one to be reckless, even in the middle of a war. And Erikson wouldn't be doing this if he wasn't confident that he could win."

"I know... I just..." He sighed and tried to push his worries away. "I wish I could be out there with you."

"I know. But you have an important job to do here. I'd even say a much harder job."

Pitor laughed. "If Kendra asks any more difficult questions, I might run out of here and join you at the front." As humorous as that idea was, he knew that it was important to keep Kendra safe. Someone had to stay behind to take care of her, and it might as well be the person who wasn't the best fighter.

"I'm sure you'll be fine," Fitz said. "Just concentrate on

what you have to do, and I'll concentrate on what I have to do. As much as I know you wish you controlled everything, some things are out of your hands." He gave Pitor a quick kiss. "Now, can we change the subject? There's been a lot of talk about war this evening, and I'd like something lighter to think about."

"What would you suggest?"

He paused for thought. "Perhaps we could attempt to make something from that cookbook Jaya gave us?"

Pitor burst out laughing. "I think that would be a terrible idea." Jaya was an amazing cook, and he was pretty certain that she'd only given them that cookbook as a joke. Every recipe had at least twenty ingredients and thirty steps, and the last time they'd tried to make one of the dishes, they'd splattered sauce over most of the kitchen.

Fitz raised an eyebrow. "So, you're in?"

"Of course I'm in."

CHAPTER 3

There were a lot of things Kendra didn't like about today, like having to wake up early, before the sun had risen. Even though it was now bright outside, she knew that if today had been a normal day, she'd still be in bed. Another thing she didn't like was how quiet and grim everyone's mood was. Usually the mornings were full of movement and noise, with breakfast being made, lunches being packed, Mommy wondering why she could never remember where she put anything, and Mama repeatedly asking if everyone was ready. Kendra preferred those kinds of mornings.

She frowned as she waited for her mothers to finish getting ready. She'd been ready to go for a long time, but they were taking forever. Normally Mama would pull her long purple hair into a ponytail, but today she was taking forever putting it into a bun, adding lots of pins to make sure every single hair was secure. Mommy kept moving from room to room, muttering to herself about making sure everything was ready. They weren't even paying much attention to her.

At least she didn't have to wear anything special. She was allowed to wear jeans and a t-shirt while her parents had to dress in the dark blue uniform of the Tecken army. The uniforms had only ever been worn for important occasions, and Kendra used to think that they were to make everyone look official and not to actually fight in. They didn't look very comfortable.

When her mothers were finally ready, the three of them left the house. Normally one or both of them would walk Kendra to school, but she wasn't going there today. There wasn't going to be any school today and probably not tomorrow or the next day, or the day after. Her classmates would be staying at home or going to a neighbour's house with other kids, while their parents left to protect the island. Some of her classmates were happy to not have classes, but Kendra didn't mind school. Sometimes it was boring, but she never felt bad about going there. Normally she wouldn't feel bad about visiting Pitor, but today she knew that once they reached his house her mothers would go away, and she didn't want that to happen.

Her mothers had spent days trying to explain what would happen today, but they weren't very good at it. They knew when they'd be meeting up with the rest of the army, but they couldn't tell her when they'd be back. They knew that they'd be protecting the part of the island where the bridge to Stanton used to be, but didn't know if they'd have to actually fight. They didn't know how much fighting Fitz would have to do once he reached Stanton or when he'd come back, or how long the fighting would last or if they'd win. All this uncertainty was making Kendra more nervous than she'd ever felt before.

The short walk to her uncles' house was usually pleasant, but today it felt like there was a dark shadow over everything. The streets were quieter, and there were large tents around the island that rose higher than the houses and made her feel like she was in some kind of box. Even the bright blue sky didn't look the same.

Pitor and Fitz were waiting for them outside their home. Pitor was dressed casually in a button-up shirt and jeans, but

Fitz was wearing the same dark blue uniform as her mothers, and his green hair had been neatly combed back. They walked down the front steps to greet Kendra, and their footsteps seemed heavier than usual. Kendra didn't pay attention as the four of them talked. She just wanted this fight to be over and her mothers and Fitz to be home and for everything to go back to the way it was.

"Be a brave girl for Mommy," Alix said, kneeling down and kissing Kendra on her cheek.

Kendra promised she would, but the unhappy look never left her face. She didn't want to be brave -- she wanted everything to go back to normal.

"You always have to be up at the front..." Pitor said quietly, entwining his fingers with Fitz's.

"You always say you love my strength of conviction," Fitz replied.

Pitor smiled in spite of himself. "You always know the wrong thing to say."

Fitz returned the smile and kissed him. "I'll be back soon."

"You'd better."

Jaya playfully mussed up Kendra's hair. "Keep Uncle Pitor company until we get back, sweetie. We don't want him to be sad that he can't join us, so you have to take care of him, okay?"

Kendra fought hard to keep the frown on her face. "Yes, Mama."

"Good girl," Jaya said, kissing her on top of her head.

Alix gave Kendra once last hug before standing up. "We'll be back as soon as possible."

Pitor held onto his husband's hand until Fitz finally had to leave, their arms stretching out so that they could maintain contact for as long as possible. He watched them walk away, and only after they had disappeared from sight did he swallow his fears.

"Would you like to play a game?" he asked Kendra, keeping his voice light and playful.

Kendra shook her head. She was still staring down the street, where her mothers had been. "When will they be back?"

"I don't know."

"I want them back now."

He put his hand on her shoulder. "Your mothers have gone away many times before. This is no different."

"But it is," she said, her voice shaking.

Pitor knelt down in front of Kendra. "I know that this is scary, but I'm not worried. Do you know why?"

She shook her head again.

"I know that they're going to be okay, because our side has a secret weapon." He smiled brightly, pushing away all his doubts and fears. "Do you remember the story we read about the Six-Elemental, and how strong he was and how he could use all six elements and not just one?"

She nodded. "But I thought he wasn't real."

"That's what we all thought. But then we found someone just like him, who can control all six elements. The good news is that she's on our side. She's going to fight for us and make sure that all of our families and friends come home safe."

Kendra's grey eyes widened. "Really? She's going to protect my Mama and Mommy and Fizy?"

He nodded. "So, you don't have to worry. Magnus Erikson has been preparing for this battle for a long time, and with the Six-Elemental on our side, we'll easily win this fight."

CHAPTER 4

Hours after the fighting began, the war was over.

Magnus Erikson had given the Cambrian Forces enough time to set up barricades around Stanton, but their preparation was in vain, just as he'd predicted. After the Six-Elemental used the power of Earth to create a bridge, Erikson successfully led the Tecken Army onto Stanton and began gaining ground at an alarming rate. The Forces tried their best to hold the Army back, but the Six-Elemental was stronger than they had anticipated, using her powers to burst through their barricades as if they'd been made of wet paper.

It was looking as if Erikson would have Stanton under his control by the end of the day. From there, it was only a matter of time before he took control of the other islands and finally achieved what his ancestors had so long desired – control over the entire Segment.

Then the tide suddenly turned. The Six-Elemental disappeared from the battle and before long, rumours started spreading that she had changed sides. Neither side knew what to believe, but everyone knew that whichever side she was on would win this war. The Tecken Army wondered what could have happened to make her change her mind halfway through the fight, and if it was possible that she had turned traitor after she'd fought so hard for them. The Forces wondered if this was a ploy by Erikson to give them false hope and make them drop their guard. They knew that the Six-Elemental had been on their side before she was abducted and brainwashed by Erikson's army, but they'd also watched her take down many of their soldiers. As helpful as it would be to have her power back on their side and away from Erikson, they knew that it would take a lot of effort to break the hold Tecken had on her mind.

When the Six-Elemental finally appeared, she destroyed one of the Force's barricades, allowing the Tecken Army to advance further, and proving that she was still on Erikson's side. The Army could smell their triumph in the air as they surged forward with renewed energy, ready to conquer this island. The Forces were dismayed, but they were determined to never give up, preparing to fight until the bitter end.

But just as quickly as Tecken's triumph began, it ended. It had all been a ruse – the Six-Elemental had in fact switched sides and was working with the Forces again. She used the destruction of the barricade to gain Tecken's trust, getting close enough to Erikson to murder him and end the Erikson lineage. After that, she went back to the main fight and collapsed the ground underneath herself and the Tecken Army, taking them down singlehandedly.

When the dust cleared, the war was over. Magnus Erikson had been defeated.

The Cambrian Forces had won.

CHAPTER 5

When Pitor picked up Kendra after school, there was a scowl on her face. Usually she was happy to see him, but even after Pitor smiled and said hello, the scowl remained.

"Bad day?" he asked gently.

"I don't like it anymore," she huffed. "Too many changes."

Pitor made a sympathetic sound and gently ruffled her hair. She scowled even harder, and the look on her face made him laugh out loud. His laughter caused her to laugh and the scowl finally disappeared.

"Let's talk about it at home, okay?" Pitor said.

"Fine..."

As they walked, he tried to keep Kendra distracted by talking about anything but school. Although this was supposed to be a new time of peace and understanding, he knew how dangerous it could be to voice an opinion against the changes being made. The official line from the Inter-Segment Security offices was that they were not here to punish anyone, but Pitor had no doubt that they were taking down the names of anyone displaying resistance.

Pitor knew enough about military strategy to prepare himself for the inevitable appearance of the Inter-Segment Security team, the government that ruled each island and reported back to the Council of Twelve. The very first thing the ISS did was to reclaim the building in the centre of the island and set up their headquarters inside.

Pitor was glad that the residents of Tecken had been fore-warned of the battle's loss, as it had given them time to secure important items that would have surely be destroyed by the ISS. This warning had come from Akola Allen, the current Leader of Tecken. She had been one of Erikson's most trusted soldiers and witnessed the Six-Elemental's betrayal and Erikson's final moments. She knew that without him, it would only be a matter of time before the war ended and the ISS showed up, so she returned to Tecken, choosing to avoid a pointless battle in favour of preparing the island's inhabitants for what was to come.

As months went on, the ISS followed almost every step that Pitor thought they would. Admittedly, he was a bit surprised when they appointed Allen to be the Leader of Tecken, but there were certain advantages to the decision. Not only was she Tecken-born, which showed that the ISS wasn't keen on taking complete control of the island, but she was one of the few people on Tecken who would deign to deal with them.

Although Pitor understood war and its inevitable aftermath, Kendra was a child who didn't. She didn't quite understand what was happening or why, but she knew that things were changing, and she did not like it one bit. His assignment to look after her meant that he had to stop her from voicing her opinions in public and getting put on a watch-list. It would have been easier if she had been a teenager, but she was only six years old.

When they reached his house, Pitor led her into the kitchen and poured two glasses of apple juice.

"Now, tell me what happened at school," he said, handing her one of the glasses.

The scowl returned to Kendra's face. "I wanted to read the story of how Titus blew up the bridges and made the island safe for us, but it's not in the library. Now there are a bunch of stupid stories about other islands, but I don't want to read those! I wanna read about us!"

Pitor put a serious look on his face. "I understand exactly how you're feeling."

"You do?" she asked.

"Of course. A lot has changed in the past month."

The ISS had started removing books, songs, and movies that were Erikson-related, in favour of bringing in items that promoted inclusion and peace. The official word was that anything that did not promote hate or violence would be returned, but Pitor knew that most of those items would never see the light of day again.

"I don't like it. I want things back the way they were." She angrily crossed her arms.

"A lot of us feel that way, but unfortunately that's not going to happen any time soon."

"Why?"

Pitor took in a deep breath. "Do you remember after your Mommy and Mama came back from fighting, how we explained to you that there were going to be many changes coming soon and that we all needed to be patient?"

"Can't we just *not* change anything?"

He shook his head. "No, because Magnus Erikson is not in charge anymore. Someone else is our Leader, and she has to be nice to the people making the changes. If she's not nice, then they'll remove her and put one of their own people in her place. And we don't want that. If that happened, things would get even worse."

"That's stupid."

He nodded, taking a drink of juice to buy some time as he thought of an appropriate reply. "It's how things are now," he said gently. "We lost the fight. The people who won get to make up the rules, and we have to follow them."

Kendra sighed. "Why not fight again until we win?"

"Because the Six-Elemental is helping the other side now, and as long as she's with them, we can't win. She's too powerful."

"She's stupid. I hate her."

"So do a lot of us..." Pitor took another drink and waited as she tried to process everything he'd told her.

"I don't like it," she grumbled. "I wanna read what I wanna read."

"Well, luckily I can help you with that," he smiled.

Her eyes opened wide. "How?"

"I have some of those stories you like right here, at home. If you want to read them, you can do so whenever you come over. And if there are any stories I don't have, let me know and I'll try to find them."

"Yay!" she clapped her hands in excitement.

"But, first," he leaned closer to her, "you must promise me two things."

She settled down and her eyes widened with curiosity.

"First, you must never tell anyone else about the books I have – not even your mothers. This has to be our secret. If the wrong people found out about these stories, then they would come in here and take all of them away, and we'd never be able to read them ever again."

"I promise." She nodded emphatically and made a cross motion over her heart.

"And secondly, you must try to control your feelings. I know that this is a difficult and scary time, but getting angry will solve nothing. If you feel angry about something, put those feelings aside until you talk to me."

"...Okay..." she promised, not quite as enthusiastically as before.

"Good!" Pitor's smile appeared again, brighter than before. "Now let's go get that book for you!"

He led her upstairs, to his office. Letting go of her hand, he walked over to the bookshelf, took a box from the bottom, and opened it. As he dug through the books inside, Kendra wandered around the room, picking up random objects and examining them before putting them back down.

"Do you ever get angry?" Kendra asked.

"Sometimes," he answered honestly. "But I know that it isn't helpful, so I try to turn that anger into something useful. Like collecting all the books they don't want us to have and keeping them safe."

Kendra went back to her exploring. A few seconds later, Pitor found the book and lifted it triumphantly out of the box, but before he could announce his success, Kendra spoke up again.

"Do you ever get sad?"

He turned around and saw that she was holding a wooden frame. He didn't have to see the picture inside to know that it was of his wedding day to Fitz. It showed the two of them standing together, arms around each other as the sun set in the background. His reply caught in his throat, and he could feel a tightness around his heart that appeared every time he thought of his late husband. He couldn't help remembering how he had sat with Kendra and her mothers, waiting for Fitz to come home from the war, watching the minutes turn into hours, knowing deep inside that something wasn't right.

"Sometimes," he answered quietly. "Most times."

"I miss him," Kendra said, tears welling up in her eyes.

Pitor put the book down and went over to her, wrapping her in a hug. "I know. But we should be thankful that we had as much time with him as we did."

"But I wanted more."

Tears began to fill his own eyes. "Me too, Kendra. Me too."

CHAPTER 6

The sigh Kendra let out was loud enough for Pitor to hear from the kitchen. He put down his pen and walked over to the doorway between the kitchen and living room. For the past half hour, Kendra had been lying on the couch, staring at the ceiling, moping. When he'd asked her mothers if she could stay with him while they went away, it had been in the hopes of discussing something important with her, but her current attitude wasn't encouraging.

"I'm old enough to stay home alone by myself," she said, talking to him for the first time since she'd arrived at his house.

Pitor laughed to himself and leaned against the wall. "Is this your way of telling me that you're too cool to hang out with your uncle?"

"No, I just..." She sat up and looked at him over the back of the couch. "It's just one weekend. It's not like I'd burn the house down or anything."

Pitor put an overly serious expression on his face. "I didn't want to say this, but I begged your mothers to let you stay here this weekend. I'm such an old, lonely man, Kendra, and the only joy I feel is when you visit." His lower lip trembled, as if he was about to start crying.

Kendra scoffed and rolled her eyes. "You're such a liar."

Pitor shrugged off his fake-sadness. "Just trying to make you laugh."

"Just trying to distract me..." She turned away from him and her gaze fell upon the mantle across the room. It was lined with photo frames, each containing a picture of Fitz, either alone or with Pitor or her mothers or her. In the centre of the frames was a small black box with a polished metal ring resting on top. Guilt started to build up inside of her as she realized that Pitor probably was an old, lonely man who appreciated her visits. "Have you ever thought of getting married again?" she asked him.

He didn't answer right away, and she was worried that she'd said something inappropriate. She tried to think of something – anything – to say to change the subject.

"Not yet," Pitor replied, trying to keep his voice light. "Maybe someday – but not yet."

"But it's been nine years. Don't you get..." she trailed off. "Never mind. Forget I asked."

Pitor walked over to the mantle and picked up one of the frames. It held the first picture he had taken of his late husband, during their third date. Fitz was trying to look alluring but was having a hard time staying serious. It made for an extremely adorable picture.

"I know that a lot of time has passed," he said, smiling sadly, "and that Fitz would want me to move on, but I'm not ready to let him go."

"I'm sorry I asked."

He put the picture back on the mantle and turned to Kendra. "It's okay to be curious, and don't think that you can't ask me anything. The only thing I don't want you doing is worrying about me. I may be stubborn, but I'm doing fine. Now, how'd you like to stop sulking and do something productive?"

"I've already done my homework."

"Then how about helping me? I'm putting together a collection of Elina's speeches after she took over leadership from Titus."

Kendra stood up from the couch and followed him into the kitchen. "Aren't you scared that someone will find out about your collections and all the Erikson books you have?"

"Of course not. Only people I trust know about them."

"But can your judgement really be trusted?" she teased. "You told me about your books when I was, like, five."

"Six. And you never told anyone, not even your mothers." He sat down in front of his notepad. "Despite what the ISS tells us, the number of people on Tecken who want to see our past preserved is much larger than you would think. We know how important it is to keep these books safe."

Kendra sat down across from him and looked at the pile of books on the table. "You know, in school they're not even teaching us about the real events that led to the First Invasion. There's nothing about Magnus the First's disdain for the way that the Council was ruling the Segment, or for the way Humanists were treating Elementals like crap. It's like, just because the Humanists are lying low now, we can overlook the fact that they used to be terrible."

"History is written by the victors..." Pitor said softly. Now that most of their literature had disappeared from public view, he saw it as his responsibility to not just keep these texts safe, but to make them available to others. He spent his free time copying sections for others to read, as well as compiling his own collections. The ISS would lock him up if they knew what he was doing, but Pitor planned to never let them find out.

He opened his mouth to say something, but quickly changed his mind. Instead he pushed a small pile of books over to Kendra. "See if you can find any of Elina's speeches in these. Mark any you find with a bookmark, so I'll know where to go next."

"Sure." Kendra sighed and opened the first book, but after flipping through a few pages she stopped and looked up. "You should teach a secret history class. You know all about the Eriksons and both Invasions. You'd be a great teacher."

"I'm afraid that it would be too risky," he replied. "If the ISS found a group of us gathered together, learning about the history of the Eriksons, they'd stop the class and everyone in attendance would be in trouble."

"But what's the worst they could do? They couldn't arrest you. People wouldn't allow it."

He shrugged. "We don't know what they would do or how far they'd go to stop us. I, for one, don't intend to find out. Trust me, it's better to fly under the radar for the time being. When the time to retake this island is at hand, we will make ourselves known."

Kendra paused, her eyes widening. "Is someone planning on taking back the island?" A grin broke out on her face and she leaned closer.

Pitor attempted to play coy. "Well, Erikson may be dead, but his ideals still survive."

"But who's going to lead? There aren't any more Eriksons..." her voice trailed off as she thought of every logical possibility. "Is it one of the Drakes? They're always trying to make themselves seem more important – especially now." She sat up and snapped her fingers. "I bet it's Illiana Drake. She's always boasting about how her grand-uncle married Ivan Erikson, even though she's got no Erikson blood in her."

"I cannot confirm or deny anything."

Kendra frowned. "You're the one who brought this up, Pitor. Don't start what you can't finish."

He had to laugh. As a teenager, Kendra had developed quite the attitude. However, she had a point.

"The ISS think that they won the war," he began, dropping his voice low, "but we know better. This peace, especially between Humanists and Elementals, is only temporary. At some point the Humanists will revert back to their old ways and the balance will fail. When that happens, the teachings of the Eriksons will surface again, and those of us who appear to have been defeated will rise up."

She sighed, disappointed. "But that could take forever. You could be waiting decades."

Pitor shrugged again. "I happen to be a very stubborn old man."

This would be the perfect time for him to tell her what he needed to say, but for some reason the words stuck in his mouth. Despite all his knowledge, he wasn't certain of how she would take the news, and he knew that once he said it out loud, there would be no going back.

Kendra looked at the book in her hands, but it no longer held her attention. She stood up and poured herself a glass of water, unable to stop thinking about a future uprising and restoring Tecken to its former glory.

"The Humanists would have to be idiots to do anything while the Six-Elemental is still around," she said, leaning against the counter. "She's the reason they're lying low right now. And she could live to be a hundred, for all we know."

For as long as she could remember she'd hated the Six-Elemental. Not only was Kit Tyler responsible for the defeat of the Tecken army and the death of Magnus Erikson, but also the death of Fitz. He had been one of the soldiers who'd died in final battle, when the Six-Elemental showed her true colours and turned her powers on the Tecken army and herself.

"She should have been the one who died that day," Kendra said quietly.

Pitor couldn't help nodding in agreement. Memories started to fill his thoughts, but he pushed them out of his mind and tried to stay focused on the matter at hand.

Over the past nine years, he had made sure to inform Kendra of Tecken's history. He'd provided her with books, the subjects getting more serious and political as she grew older, and helped fill in any blanks in the new ISS curriculum, teaching her the actual history that the teachers were leaving out or modifying. Kendra was a smart kid and held a lot of contempt for the ISS and their meddling, although she'd long ago learned to control her disdain. In other words, she was growing up just fine. Pitor only hoped that she'd be able to handle what he was about to tell her.

"Kendra, what are your plans after high school?" he asked.

She shrugged and walked back over to the table. "Maybe go into teaching, like Mom."

"You don't sound very sure about that."

"That's because of the stupid ISS. I'd like to teach our real history, but they'd never let me." She put her elbows on the table and rested her chin in one hand. "What else am I gonna do? I can't be a writer, because I'll never be able to write what I really want. And Mama gave up on teaching me how to cook ages ago."

It was now or never.

Pitor took in a deep breath. "I was hoping that you might want to do something a bit... more with your life."

She gave him an unimpressed look.

"And by that," he elaborated, "I was thinking that maybe you'd want to go into public relations. Learn how the islands work, and how to handle matters with the public. And maybe, eventually, become our island's Leader."

"Why would I want to do that?"

"Because leadership is in your blood."

Her look became even more unimpressed, which Pitor had thought would be difficult, but she achieved it with ease.

"Who cares what's in my blood?" she scoffed. "And why should it matter? Leadership's about aptitude, not genetics."

"Well, Allen won't be able to lead the island forever, and I'd prefer for her successor to be someone who respects our history and knows how to manoeuvre around the ISS."

"And for some weird reason you want that person to be me? Random..."

Pitor paused. "It's not as random as you would think. See, I know your parents."

"Of course you do, you've been friends for, like, ever."

"No," he cleared his throat. "Your *biological* parents."

Kendra sat up straighter. "What? But how?"

He took in a breath. "After your adoption, I was asked by your biological father to keep an eye on you. He was unable to raise you, but wanted to make sure that someone was watching out for you at all times. It made sense to ask me, since I was friends with your mothers."

She shook her head, unable to believe what she was hearing. Why would her biological father recruit someone to look after her? And how was he able to find out where she had been placed? Her mothers had told her years ago that her file had been sealed by her biological parents, and only their medical information was available for viewing. How could Pitor know who her father was?

"But that doesn't make sense," she said. "Unless..." she looked up at Pitor, her grey eyes widening. "Are you...?"

He quickly shook his head. "No, not me. Someone... more

important."

She shook her head again, trying to halt all further ideas along this line of thinking, as if it would stop her mind from arriving at a destination she didn't want to reach. "Pitor, if this is some kind of joke, it's not funny. You need to stop."

"It's not a joke." He stood up and leaned on the table. "I wanted to tell you sooner, but I had to make sure that you were old enough to understand."

"But why bother telling me at all?" she said, her voice rising in anger. "What if I don't want to know? What if I don't care? What does it matter who my biological parents are?"

"It matters because you are the only child of Magnus Erikson the Second!"

The silence that followed lasted over a minute. Neither of them moved, both rooted to the ground by the sudden revelation.

"No," Kendra said, breaking the silence as she rose to her feet. "Erikson never had a kid. He never married. Why would you say something like that? That's a horrible lie to tell someone."

"It's not a lie," Pitor replied gently. "Erikson never married, but he did have a child."

"With who?"

"Her bloodline's not important. All you need to know is that he was too preoccupied with his duties to raise you, so you were put up for adoption. The truth was kept secret from almost everyone, because he wanted you to grow up normally."

Kendra put her hands to her head and started pacing. "No. It's not true. It can't be. If I was actually his child, why would he give me away? The Eriksons are all about bloodlines and continuing the family lineage, so why wouldn't he want me to grow up to be one of them? Why hide me?"

Pitor paused and considered his answer carefully. "Okay, I may have embellished the growing up normal bit, because I didn't want to get into the real reason."

She glared at him, and he knew that holding back wouldn't be a good idea.

"He kept you a secret because the islanders would insist that he marry your biological mother, and he didn't want to be put in that situation. He didn't love her."

"He liked her enough to get her pregnant," Kendra shot back.

"Love isn't a pre-requisite for sex." Pitor realized what he'd said, and a look of horror crossed his face. "But if you want to be a kind person, you should definitely like someone enough before having sex with them. And never let anyone pressure you into doing that before you're ready."

She threw her head back and let out a frustrated groan. "I've heard this talk already from both my mothers! Get back to the Erikson-apparently-being-my-father thing!"

"Kendra, it's okay. Knowing this doesn't change who you are."

The look she gave him inferred that he was an idiot. "Pitor, if I'm Erikson's kid, then it *definitely* changes who I am. If people found out, they'd make me be an Erikson. Heck, the ISS would probably find a reason to shove me in prison for the rest of my life."

He carefully approached her. "There are only four people who know this, including you, and we won't say anything. Nobody will find out unless you want them to, and nobody can force you to be anything you don't want to be. However... You should consider that even if you weren't an Erikson, you're still one of the best people to lead this island. You know our history, you care about the people, and you know how to play the game with the ISS. Obviously, your grades would have to get better, but I know you can do that."

She sat down and put her head on the table. "I. Can't. Deal. With. This."

He had a lot more to say, but he had a feeling that words wouldn't help right now. Instead, he left her alone and went up to his office. It would be best to give her some time to absorb what had been said. If she wanted to talk about it further, he'd gladly discuss everything, but if she wanted to forget all about it, then there was nothing he could do.

Maybe it had been the wrong time to bring this up. He should have waited until her eighteenth birthday, but that wasn't for another three years. Besides, she was doing well in school but not great, and she needed to pick up her grades. Pitor suspected that Kendra was holding herself back on purpose, as some kind of rebellion against the ISS, and he wanted to give her a reason to take school seriously so that she'd be able to achieve her full potential.

The truth was that he needed her to accept this. With him guiding her, she could easily take over leadership of Tecken and bring this island back to its former glory. The resistance needed time to rebuild itself, but it also needed to know that it was building towards something. Illiana Drake was trying to fill the void left by Magnus Erikson's death, but Pitor didn't see the point of having a distant relative pick up the mantle when there was a true-blooded heir right in front of them. This island needed someone more suited to leadership than Illiana. It needed an Erikson.

Pitor tried to continue his work upstairs, keeping an ear out for any sounds from the first floor. As he searched through his books, he could hear Kendra occasionally letting out frustrated noises. There had been no coherent words, which wasn't good, but at least she wasn't breaking things.

He was halfway through the second book when he realized that it had been a while since he'd heard anything. There had been no sound of the front door opening and closing, so she couldn't have left the house. Pitor wondered if he should go downstairs and try to talk to her again, but he couldn't think of anything more to say. Maybe it would be best to pretend the whole thing hadn't happened.

"Pitor..."

He nearly dropped the book in his hands. Turning, he saw Kendra standing in the doorway. Somehow she'd made it up the stairs without him hearing her.

"Pitor," she began again, her voice heavy with emotion. "I need to know if you're telling me the truth. I need to hear you say that this is one hundred percent true, that I am definitely Magnus Erikson's daughter. Because if you're lying and I find out, I will never, ever forgive you."

Pitor took a deep breath. "It's true. You are the only child of Magus Erikson, born out of wedlock, and hidden away. And I believe that you are our best hope for uniting all of Tecken, and taking back our island."

Kendra looked down at the floor, unable to respond. She'd hoped that this was a joke or some kind of elaborate lie. Never before had she thought of herself as a leader, or as anything more than the daughter of Alix and Jaya Chen. To find out that Magnus Erikson was her father...

But why should it matter who she shared her EDNA with? If Magnus had wanted her to be an Erikson, then he should have acknowledged her, not kept her hidden away like some shameful secret. What would've happened to her if he'd had a legitimate heir? Would she never have found out the truth? Would Pitor be asking some other person to be Tecken's Leader? How much did she owe to a father who was never there for her?

As angry as she was at Magnus, her thoughts turned to the people of Tecken. She loved her island and wanted the best for everyone on it. The loss of the war and the ISS's takeover had led to hard lives for everyone who'd enjoyed freedom under the Erikson's rule. She wasn't the only person who wished that things could go back to the way they used to be.

But was Pitor right that she would be the best person for the job? It was true that people would follow her for being an Erikson, but she didn't want them to follow her blindly. She didn't want to be a Leader unless she was worthy of that title, and right now she wasn't sure if that was possible. Was leadership something that could be passed through blood or was it something that could be learned? Maybe under Pitor's guidance she could become worthy, but what if that never happened? What if she turned out to be nothing more than a disappointment?

"Kendra?" Pitor asked quietly. "Are you okay?"

She swallowed hard and looked up at him. "Tell me what I need to do."

CHAPTER 7

Even though it was Kendra's first time in this particular room, there was a certain familiarity to it. The two beds were in the same location as the beds in her old, shared dorm room at Drakkar University last year. In fact, every piece of furniture was in the same place, a set of each on opposite sides of the room, providing a perfect mirror image. She wondered if this design was standard for all Universities in the Segment, and then realized that over the next few years she'd have the opportunity to find out.

Instead of going to university on Tecken, as she'd planned to do before all of this, Pitor and she had come up with a plan to spend those four years studying throughout the Segment. Despite being well informed in both the history and current affairs of Tecken, her knowledge of the other islands was definitely lacking. If she hoped to one day lead her people, then she needed to experience what life was like on every island in the Segment. After all, it wasn't until Magnus Erikson the First saw how the other islands were being run that he realized how the current system was at fault and how he could make life better for everyone.

Last year – the first of the four – had been spent on Drakkar. It was the first time she'd been away from Tecken, but there was no time to be homesick. Not only did she have her classes to focus on, but she also needed to learn as much as she could about the island and its people. It was an eye-opening and oddly pleasant experience, and she felt a strange sort of freedom being out there all alone.

Drakkar had been easy, but she doubted that Stanton would be the same.

Unsure of when her roommate would be showing up, Kendra decided to lay claim to the left side of the room, placing her luggage on the bed. It would be practical to start unpacking, but she was feeling restless. Ever since her arrival on Stanton, she'd felt as if she was being watched. It was a ridiculous thought, because of course nobody was watching her, but she was a born-and-raised Tecken on an island that had been invaded by Tecken. Twice. No matter what kind of reconciliation thing the ISS had going on, some wounds were still too fresh.

This paranoia was why she had driven her Sol-car through Drakkar and Aesira to get here, instead of taking the more direct route from Tecken, and why she was determined not to bring up her real home to anyone. It was going to be an interesting year.

Leaving the room and her luggage behind, Kendra decided to go for a walk. It would be a good idea to orientate herself with the layout of the island and get an idea of where everything was located. Maybe once she was more familiar with the island, she'd feel less like an outsider.

The day was sunny and warm and perfect for walking around. It was early afternoon, so the sun wouldn't be setting for hours. There was still plenty of time for her to get lost and found a couple of times. Heading south, she decided to walk downtown and see if there were any good cafes or shops that this island could offer. There was nothing particularly unique about Stanton, and for the most part it looked a lot like Drakkar, with short streets, long avenues, and enough greenery to forget that the small island was surrounded on all sides by water. No matter where she was she could see the ISS building standing tall in the centre of the island. Kendra had a feeling that most residents would look upon that building favourably, but to her it felt as if it was looming, keeping watch over everything and everyone.

As she walked, she tried to pay attention to her surroundings, taking note of any stores that she might like to visit or any restaurants that tempted her. Although she wasn't heading in any particular direction, she soon found herself at the corner of 3rd Avenue and 32nd Street, and only a few blocks away from where the Second Invasion had come crashing to an end.

The history of the Second Invasion wasn't the most detailed, considering all the behind-the-scenes information that could only be gathered from first-hand interviews, and all the information that the ISS had decided to keep secret, but Pitor's teachings had filled her in on anything that might have been missing from the history books. She knew about the final moments of the Invasion, when the Tecken Army thought that they had won it all only to be betrayed at the last minute.

She would have come across this place eventually, but why did it have to be so soon? Perhaps her subconscious had led her here. Better to go now and get it out of the way, instead of avoiding it for months.

As she looked down the avenue, she went over that moment in her mind. The battle was raging on at the third barricade – Tecken's Army was feeling confident, while the Cambrian Forces were merely trying to delay the inevitable. Suddenly, out of nowhere, the Six-Elemental appeared, declared the war over, and made her final, fatal, move.

At this moment, the street looked normal and all hints of battle had been erased. People walked along the sidewalks, engrossed in conversations, cars and bikes passed through on their way to somewhere else. Life went on.

But this area – the intersection of 3rd Avenue and 35th Street – was where life had stopped for many others. The majority of those caught in the collapse survived with broken bones, internal bleeding, and cuts, but those who'd died had families and friends waiting for them – families and friends that they would never see again.

Kendra looked out at the intersection. She could almost see Fitz standing there in his blue uniform, exactly as he'd been on the day of the Second Invasion, the last time she saw him alive. He had been prepared to give his life for his island, but the death he'd been given was meaningless. She could feel her muscles tense as her hand clenched into a fist. The Six-Elemental should have done the right thing and given the Tecken Army a chance to surrender. Maybe they would have, maybe they wouldn't – but the choice would have been theirs. They could have gone down fighting, instead of being murdered by a person pretending to be their ally.

Δ

By the time Kendra returned to her dorm room, her roommate had arrived.

"I see you've claimed the left side," the young woman smiled brightly, "but don't worry, I like the right. Hi, I'm Skye Celucci."

She extended her right hand, and Kendra politely shook it.

"Kendra Chen."

Skye smiled. "That was easy! Now, I'm not going to bother calling you Chen – I'm jumping straight to Kendra. We're roommates, after all, so why bother sticking to formalities when we're obviously going to be friends? And even if we don't really like each other, it's so impersonal to be so formal. Sorry to burst your bubble if you'd planned on spending our first few days as roommates calling each other by our last names, but I always consider it a waste of time."

"Um. Sure thing... Skye."

"Excellent! And, since I know you're wondering – because everyone wonders – but I was not named because of my looks. Skye was my grandmother's name."

Kendra couldn't help smiling. With her dark green hair, tawny skin, and light grey eyes, Skye's colouring seemed more akin to a park than the actual sky.

"Are you sure your parents weren't colour-blind and lied when they were found out?" Kendra suggested.

Skye paused. "You know, I never thought of it that way. Huh..."

"Sorry to blow your mind on the first day."

"Apology accepted." She smiled brightly. "So, were you planning on unpacking or would it be preferable for us to grab a bite to eat and get all that 'getting to know you' stuff out of the way?"

Kendra had to pause for a second to collect her thoughts. "Has anyone ever told you that you're very direct?"

Her face went very serious. "Never."

Kendra knew that her roommate was messing with her. Her previous roommate on Drakkar had been nice, but he mostly kept to himself and his studies, so she wasn't expecting Skye's enthusiasm or straight-forward attitude. This roommate was going to be higher maintenance.

Skye smiled again. "You're my fourth roommate in three years, so I've learned to dispense with the whole polite conversation thing."

"Four in three years?" she whistled. "What'd you do? Kill them?"

She laughed. "The first one got homesick and moved back after the first semester. The second decided that school wasn't for them, and the third I killed. Just kidding! The third wanted to room with a friend this year."

"Impressive. You're only my second. I went to Drakkar University last year but decided that I wanted to see more of the Segment."

"Ah, which means that you'll probably run off to some other exotic island next year, so getting to know each other would be a complete waste of time. Should we call off lunch?"

Kendra pretended to consider the option. "Well, it would be a really awkward year if we ignored each other. Maybe we should go, just in case. Who knows – we might end up hating each other and looking forward to the end of the year."

Skye nodded seriously. "I like the way you think, Kendra."

They walked to a sandwich shop which was close to campus and approved by Skye – two very important details that she made sure to point out. There were other eateries that were Skye-approved but weren't as close, and she made sure to mention them on the walk. Since Kendra was new to the island, she was happy to hand the reins over. Then again, she had a feeling that the reins had been permanently glued to Skye's hands, and trying to take them away would involve a lot of pain and swearing.

Luckily, Skye's recommendation turned out to be trustworthy. It was a fair price, had a lot of great options to choose from, and the atmosphere was casual but not overly loud.

"So," Skye began, once they were seated at a table with their food, "you've come to Stanton to explore. Elaborate, if you will."

Kendra pretended to think over her words before launching into her well-rehearsed speech. "Well, I'd never let my home island before, not even for vacations, and I figured that college was the perfect time to get out there and experience living somewhere else."

"You're totally going to leave Stanton after this year," Skye muttered, frowning. "You'll leave and I'll have to move on to roommate number five. I think I'm going to have to hate you, Kendra."

She smirked. "And here I was hoping you'd like me enough not to murder me."

"We'll have to say goodbye at some time. It might as well be on my terms."

Kendra stifled a laugh. "I want to state for the record that it's alarming how casually you talk about murdering me."

"Dang, I guess I'll have to stop." Skye pretended to be sad about the decision, even wiping away an imaginary tear, but two seconds later she was back to normal. "Next question: what are you studying?"

Kendra took note of Skye's acting ability. She was going to have to be very careful over the next year. With all the quick repartee, there was a possibility that she'd say the wrong thing or contradict herself, and she had a feeling that Skye was smart enough to pick up on anything out of the ordinary.

"I'm doing a little bit of everything," Kendra answered noncommittally. "I'm hoping to get a job with the ISS after school."

"Ah, a government girl..."

"What about you? What are your job prospects?"

"Clothing design," Skye answered. "Or maybe journalism. Or mechanics – I haven't decided yet."

They continued talking while they ate, with Skye going

on about all the great things there were to do on Stanton and why a person should probably give it more than a year. Kendra learned that Skye lived with her father, but had moved onto campus to give him a better chance at dating. As Skye put it, 'I didn't want him to feel awkward about bringing someone home, if you know what I mean.' Kendra talked about living with her mothers, and how she moved to campus to get an idea of what it was like to live on her own.

Whenever Skye asked about home, Kendra avoided saying anything specific. She was careful never to mention that Drakkar was or wasn't her home – simply letting the conversation drift in that direction if a question got too involved. It was one of the things Pitor had taught her: if you're careful enough, you never actually have to lie to a person. Just phrase your words a certain way or answer abstractly enough that the person comes to their own conclusions.

Whenever the questions started to get too personal, Kendra would always turn the subject back on her roommate. She hoped that it was coming off as shy and not avoidant.

"But if you've lived on Stanton your whole life, how can you advocate not travelling?" Kendra asked after another pointed comment had been directed her way.

Sky looked as if she'd been waiting for the question to pop up. "That's the exact reason why I can be an advocate. If I've lived here my entire life and never wanted to travel, why should anyone else?"

"But you've never been anywhere else. Wouldn't you rather travel to other islands, see what they're like, and make your own decisions about each of them?"

"There's nothing to stop me from travelling for a day or a weekend. I'm just saying that you don't have to go live on every island. If you've got friends and family here, why wouldn't you stay?"

Kendra shrugged. "I think the best way to serve the people is to understand what they're going through, and how will I find that out if I don't get to see what's going on?" Skye looked like she wanted to say something, but Kendra quickly started talking again. "I mean, why should we keep doing things the way we've always been doing them if there's a better way out there? What works on Stanton might also work in Drakkar, or vice-versa."

Skye let out a sigh. "You are really suited to public service," she said, shaking her head. "And here I thought I'd gotten a cool roommate."

Kendra debated tossing one of her carrots at her. "I can be into public service and still be cool."

"Nope," Skye shook her head more fervently. "Not possible."

"Then maybe we should stop talking about politics and get back to stupid stuff like movies and music."

There was a pause as Skye considered the suggestion, giving it much more weight than it deserved. "That sounds agreeable to me. So, favourite song?"

Δ

When it was time to choose her classes, Kendra followed the plan that she had created with Pitor, taking courses that would be an asset for a well-rounded ISS employee. However, for her first semester in Stanton, she decided to make a slight change to the list. Instead of enrolling in another history course, she signed up for an architecture class. Although she had no real interest in architecture, she was compelled to sign up because Kit Tyler worked in that field. There were no delusions that the powerful Six-Elemental would show up in the class to give a lecture or that the class would visit the company she worked for, but Kendra wanted to understand her better, through any way possible.

In the years since the war, Kendra's hatred for Tyler had grown exponentially. There were so many things wrong with the world that were all Tyler's fault, and there was no doubt that it would be a better place once she was no longer in it. It would be a stupid idea to try to fight her, especially since Kendra did not yet have an element herself, but there were other ways that a person could be defeated. While she was on this island, she vowed to learn as much as possible about her enemy – every strength and every weakness.

Kendra had big plans for the future, and she had no intention of letting the Six-Elemental interfere. Not this time.

CHAPTER 8

"Get ready. We're leaving in ten minutes."

Kendra looked up from her textbook to see her roommate standing in the doorway. Obediently, she grabbed a bookmark to hold her place.

"Where are we going?" she asked, standing up. Earlier that day, Skye had run up to her, informed her that she'd be going out with the group tonight, and then disappeared without another word.

Skye gestured grandly. "We shall be partaking in the wonderful nightlife of Stanton, including visiting an infamous local bar for a few drinks and some dancing."

She raised an eyebrow. "We're going dancing?"

"You'll have plenty of time to avoid fun once you've become a public servant. Now change into something appropriate."

Even though Kendra had homework, it could wait. For the most part, Skye understood that Kendra needed to get good grades and left her to her own devices, but every now and then Skye would think of something really interesting to do and invite her to come along. Kendra didn't mind the random invitations and was happy for the distractions. She liked to joke that Skye only invited her because she was worried about her studying to partying ratio and was trying to even the scales.

Truthfully, it was a benefit to be shown the island by a person who'd lived there her entire life. Instead of wandering around, observing everything from the outside, Skye was able to give her the insider's point of view.

"What's this infamous bar we're going to?" Kendra asked as she changed her shirt.

"The Black Hole."

The name didn't ring any bells. "And why exactly is this bar so 'infamous'?"

Skye's eyes widened as she took a dramatic step into the room. "It used to have another name, but they changed it after *the incident*. It used to be called," she paused for added tension, "Fyre."

An inner bell went off and Kendra knew exactly which bar she was talking about now but pretended to still be confused. "That means nothing to me. What's this 'incident' you speak of? Did it burn down in a name-appropriate circumstance?"

"I'm talking about the disappearance of the Six-Elemental! This bar is the last place she was seen on Stanton before she marched over with the Tecken army!"

"I see," Kendra said slowly. "So, should I be worried about someone abducting me? Is that the bar's current theme? A person gets abducted every night?"

"Of course not. Are you going to change your pants?"

"Why? What's wrong with them?"

Skye gave her a flat look. "They're pants. You'll be dancing, which means that you're going to sweat. You should put on shorts or a skirt."

"But these are my dancing pants," Kendra said, trying to sound serious.

Putting her head in her hands, Skye sighed dramatically. "You're a hopeless cause, my friend."

Kendra smiled at her disappointment. "You know what's great about pants? Not only do they look good, but they also soak up sweat. You should consider changing into pants."

"Fine," she huffed, pretending to be annoyed. "You ready?"

"Yup."

Kendra followed her roommate into the hallway. The rest of the group was waiting for them near the front of the dorm. Skye's main group of friends consisted of three people – Lin, who was majoring in Journalism and loved to analyze every situation in hilarious ways; Gen, who had yet to choose a major and happened to have Intro to Architecture with Kendra; and Quinn, who was majoring in History and was the person Kendra had the most in common with. The three knew about Skye's previous roommates and so they'd been polite but unsure when Skye first introduced her, but now they were delighted whenever she joined them.

"Let's go!" Skye commanded, and the group moved out.

As they walked, Quinn informed them about the history of The Black Hole, building up the story even more dramatically than Skye had.

"It's said that the Six-Elemental's drink was spiked by Tecken spies," Quinn said, conspiratorially, "And that's how she was taken. Her friend was distracted, probably by another Tecken spy, and didn't see any of this going down."

"So we should stick together?" Gen mocked. "Is that what you're saying?"

"No," Quinn replied, rolling her eyes. "There's only ever been one abduction from this bar. And I doubt that any of us have a reason to be kidnapped by some crazy fanatic."

Kendra couldn't help smiling as they talked, but it wasn't because of the amusing dialogue. While the others hypothesized about how the incident had gone down, she knew exactly what had happened that night. They had no idea how prepared the Tecken soldiers were and how many people had been involved, even in the slightest of ways. The abduction of the Six-Elemental had been a big operation, and those soldiers had been standing by for days, waiting for an ideal opportunity.

"Honestly," Quinn continued, "there's no difference between this bar and any of the others in town, except that this bar has a minor claim to fame – which really shouldn't be something they should be bragging about."

"Agreed," Lin nodded. "It's like claiming that your sandwich once made someone sick. It's a dumb claim to fame."

"Which is exactly why we're going there!" Skye said excitedly. "It's so dumb that it's got to be amazing. Besides, if the music is terrible, I've got a backup bar."

They continued to discuss terrible marketing plans for businesses while they walked, and it helped pass the time until they made it to the bar.

Despite The Black Hole's dubious claim to fame, it was quite full and the music was actually good. As the group made their way through the crowds, Kendra tried to picture that night as it had been explained to her by Pitor. Tecken had no proof that Kit Tyler was the Six-Elemental, but the possibility was too important to ignore. When Tyler and Bryanna Kavail, both from the ISS's not-so-secret civilian team, went out one night, the solders sprang into action. Soldier 1 separated the women by asking them to dance – an offer that Kavail took her up on. Once Kavail was gone, Soldier 2 went over to talk to Tyler. Eventually those two went to the dance floor, where Soldier 3 injected her with a concealed syringe, causing her to feel dizzy. Soldier 2 guided her off the floor, sat her down, and got her a glass of water – which he drugged. Then he guided Tyler outside, where she blacked out, and Soldier 4 picked the two of them up to drive them to the base.

The ISS had made a few embellishments to their version of what had happened, playing up the underhandedness of Tecken's operation, but the truth was that it had been easy to locate Tyler and even easier to steal her right out from under the ISS.

Δ

Despite having gone for many walks along the island and exploring almost every inch, it took three months for Kendra to finally see the Six-Elemental in the flesh. Every time she went out for a walk, she kept an eye open for someone with a particular shade of blue hair, but for the longest time there had been no luck.

It made sense that Tyler would be keeping a low profile, even now. Just because eleven years had passed, it didn't mean that people had forgotten the mess she'd created. Still, Kendra kept an eye out, hoping that she would stumble upon her by chance.

When she finally saw Tyler, it was a warm, sunny afternoon and Kendra had gone for a walk downtown, taking a break from a paper that she was working on. As she wandered along the street, the colour blue caught her eye and she finally saw her – Kit Tyler, the infamous Six-Elemental. She was holding hands with a red-haired man, both of them smiling as they walked and talked.

As Kendra watched the two of them, anger rose up inside of her. What right did Tyler have to be happy? She had betrayed thousands of people, yet here she was, smiling and laughing, holding hands with someone she loved. How many people in this Segment could no longer hold onto the hands of their loved ones because of her actions? Kendra remembered how she used to walk down the street with Pitor and Fitz, each of them holding onto one of her hands, occasionally swinging her up into the air as they walked. After the war, it felt strange to not have Fitz around, as if there was something missing in her life that could never be found. And he would have been there, if it hadn't been for Tyler.

Kendra wanted to walk up to her and punch her, but now was not the time. Doing something like that would definitely jeopardize her future, and she had too many people depending on her to throw it all away in a moment of revenge.

The anger quickly subsided, but Kendra could still feel it burning deep within. This was not a rage that she would let consume her – it would feed her purpose and drive her forward. It would make sure that she never lost sight of what was important.

One day she would make Tyler pay for all that she'd done.

CHAPTER 9

When the spring semester started, Skye made sure to consistently remind Kendra about how amazing Stanton was and how terribly boring Aesira was going to seem in comparison. She highlighted all the wonderful times they'd had, the amazing places they'd eaten at, and mentioned all the incredible things they'd be able to do next year if only Kendra wasn't abandoning her. Although Kendra could easily see through Skye's scheme, she had to admit that it was working. As the weeks passed, the thought of staying looked more and more attractive, and she found herself wondering if maybe she was leaving the island too soon.

Finally Kendra decided that it was time to phone Pitor and have a talk.

"Pitor," she began, her voice friendly but firm, "you know how relations between Stanton and Tecken are very important right now?"

"Yes," he replied warily.

"Well, I feel that it would be important for me to, perhaps, stay on the island for a few more months, to continue learning and getting a feel for the inhabitants and their wants and needs. I would still be able to come home for a week after the summer semester finishes, and then go to Aesira after that."

"Oh," the relief in Pitor's voice was audible. "So, you're still planning on going to the other islands."

"Of course," she said. The thought of dropping the plan entirely hadn't even crossed her mind. "I have no real plans for the summer, so I figured that it would be beneficial to stay here longer."

"Well, if you think staying in Stanton would be a good idea, then I defer to your judgement."

"Thanks, Pitor."

Despite his formal tone, she knew that he was okay with her decision. He usually agreed with her, but she'd never strayed very far from their plan so his ability to let go had never been truly tested. Although he made it sound as though she was in charge of what she did and where she went, she wasn't sure how he'd react if she ever wanted to do something he disagreed with.

Skye, meanwhile, was over the moon with excitement.

"This is so amazing!" she exclaimed, bouncing around the room. "I can't believe I got you to stay!"

"Well, it wasn't just you," Kendra interjected.

"Of course it was! We're going to have so much fun! How many courses are you going to take?"

"Three. Two classes and an independent study."

Skye let out a happy squeal. "That's excellent! That'll give us plenty of time for adventures!"

"Really?" Kendra paused. "I thought you'd be taking four or five classes, to make up for the time when you hadn't figured out your major."

She scoffed. "That was before you decided to stay. I can make up the other classes later. Besides, I'm not sure if biology is right for me, so I might need to change my major again. Okay, we need to think of the best things to do in Stanton during the summer..." She started talking to herself as she paced around the room.

While Skye busied herself making plans, Kendra thought about what kind of summer this would be. Being on Stanton was like living in a history book. There were plaques and memorials for the First and Second Invasions, and the streets she walked along had once been walked by Magnus Erikson – the first *and* the second. Perhaps it was the many history courses she had taken and the stories Pitor had told her, but Kendra appreciated being able to experience this history first-hand. Besides, what she had told him was true – relations between Stanton and Tecken were a very important issue and one that she needed to be prepared to handle. It made sense to spend more time here than on any other island.

She also had to admit that Skye was a part of why she was staying. As the semester passed, Kendra realized how much she would miss her roommate once she was gone. Skye's high-level, spontaneous energy was a wonderful change from the rigorous, focused schedule she had been living for the past few years. In a highly planned out life it was refreshing to have a touch of unpredictability.

"We need to go out and celebrate!"

Skye's words brought Kendra back to reality. "Huh?"

"We need ice cream! Let's go!"

Skye grabbed her hand, and Kendra allowed herself to be pulled out of the room. As Skye talked excitedly about the great times ahead, Kendra couldn't keep the smile off her face. Last summer she had spent her days working in the local library and helping Pitor with his collections, which was like a second job. Suddenly she realized that staying in Stanton would mean being away from Pitor's library. A week of reading before going to Aesira wouldn't make up for three months away from the history of her biological family. Her next summer was supposed to be spent in Cambria, so she wouldn't be able to go home then, either.

Uncertainty washed over her. Was she making a mistake? Had she allowed her feelings to take over and cause her to act rashly? Was staying on Stanton actually a terrible idea? What more could she learn here that she hadn't already learned in the past eight months?

The thought of learning something new snapped her out of the downward spiral she'd suddenly fallen into. This summer would not be a waste – she wouldn't allow it. As much as she loved reading all the books Pitor had collected, she knew that it was equally important to be out in the world, interacting with other people. She was overreacting, plain and simple. Stepping off the planned route had caused her to have a small panic attack, but she was over it now. Everything was going to work out fine.

Luckily Skye hadn't noticed this mental crisis, which took less than ten seconds to go through. They reached the ice cream shop, made their purchases, and talked more about all the fun things they'd be able to do this summer. Ice cream cones in hand, they strolled along the streets, with Skye pointing out all the places they'd have to visit.

As they walked, a flash of blue caught Kendra's attention, and she couldn't help her head snapping to the side to follow it. It was not Tyler, but that one small moment was enough to assure Kendra that she was making the right decision. Determination rose inside of her, quieting any remaining doubts. She still had plenty of work to do on Stanton.

Δ

It was yet another beautiful summer day. The weather wasn't any different than back on Tecken, but for some reason

Kendra was able to appreciate everything more here. Maybe it was because of all the turmoil that had happened. This island and its people had been through so much, and it was incredible how peaceful everything was. It wasn't the bright blue sky or the fluffy white clouds – it was the fact that two wars had been fought on this island and still life thrived.

There was plenty of time for her to enjoy the summer weather, as she was only taking two actual classes – the history class she'd forgone in the first semester, and a philosophy class about the Six-Elemental. The independent project she'd mentioned to Skye wasn't actually a class at the university, it was a personal project – one that she was currently working on as she sipped her tea and watched the building across the street. It was shortly after five o'clock and a group of employees were leaving for the day. Within that group were people of all shapes, sizes, and colours, but there was only one employee of Skyline Architects that Kendra cared about.

The more she learned about the Six-Elemental, the more she realized that Pitor's plan of reclaiming Tecken would never come to fruition as long as Tyler was around. As much as Kendra hoped for a peaceful transition of power this time around, she knew there was a chance that she would have to fight, like her family before her. Even if Tyler had publicly declared that she didn't want to be a part of the ISS, there was no guarantee that she'd stay neutral should another conflict arise. And she'd already murdered one Erikson...

Pitor didn't seem to think that this was anything to worry about, but Kendra wasn't going to risk letting the people of Tecken down because she was too stubborn to acknowledge a threat.

During her 'independent study', she followed Tyler, taking copious amounts of notes. Most of the time, Tyler wore a hat over her hair, making it difficult to spot her, but Kendra soon became adept at recognizing her efforts to hide in public. There had been a few occasions where Tyler didn't cover up her hair, but those only happened when she was out with someone else. Whenever she was alone, she tried her best to blend in. She also usually wore clothing that covered most of her elemental Tattoos, despite the warm weather.

It was rare to see Tyler outside of her commute to work. Most days, the best Kendra could hope for was to catch a glimpse of her on her way in or out of the building. Sometimes Tyler went out with friends, but she rarely went out alone. Although Kendra couldn't keep an eye on her all the time, she recorded everything she saw, knowing that even the tiniest detail might be beneficial in the future.

As Kendra's notes grew, she started to come to the realization that the Six-Elemental was not an all-powerful, mythical beast – she was simply a person. Yes, she had more power than anyone else, but that didn't mean that she was invincible. Every person had their weak spot, and Kendra was getting closer to finding out what Tyler's was.

Δ

"I can't believe you're leaving me," Skye groaned. She was lying on her bed, one arm flung over her eyes. "After all the effort I put into making you cool…"

"Sorry," Kendra replied, trying to sound sad and failing, "but you knew it would never work out. I'm into public relations…"

"And I'm into cool stuff. So, what's next on the grand Segment tour?" she asked, removing her arm and looking over at Kendra, who was still packing despite her many protestations.

She smiled. "Aesira. I'm going to roam the farmlands in my spare time."

"Lame. Seriously, Kendra, could you be any more boring? I should have tried harder to make you less of a dork."

She laughed. "I'll be sure to write you and keep you up to date on all my lame goings-on."

"And I will write you to let you know that I'm still cool and tell you about all the fun stuff I'm doing that you're not."

"I look forward to reading your letters."

"Spoken like a true public servant." Skye sighed loudly.

Kendra hid her laughter and continued to pack. Luckily she hadn't accumulated much while in Stanton. Changing islands every year meant packing light, and it didn't take long for her to finish. Soon she'd be on the road to Tecken, and then on to another island.

"I guess all those nights of whispering suggestions that you stay on Stanton into your ear while you slept were a waste of time…"

Kendra looked up from her bags. She opened her mouth to ask Skye if she was telling the truth or kidding, but then decided against it. There was a strong possibility that this was true, and if that were the case then she'd rather not know. Some questions were better off not being answered.

"I'm sure you'll do fine without me," she replied. "Your next roommate will probably be much cooler."

"Or they might be a thief. Or a murderer. Or another public servant!" Skye sighed again.

"Well, you could always come with me to Aesira," Kendra remarked. As soon as the words were out of her mouth she realized what she'd said. While it would be nice to have a friend along, especially with everything being new all over again, she wasn't supposed to be inviting people to join her. And if Skye actually did come with her to Aesira, what would she say about her choice of school the year after?

"No thanks," Skye scoffed. "Aesira's *super* boring. But you'll find out soon enough. Let me know when you decide to go to school on a cooler island and maybe I'll join you."

Kendra turned away, pretending to double-check her packing, but it was mostly to hide her relief. It would have been difficult to keep up the facade for a second year. However, she was also disappointed. It had been fun to have a friend again. After learning about her family, Kendra started to drift away from her school friends on Tecken. They were all going about their lives normally, but she had a higher purpose – one that they couldn't know about yet. Pitor was great, but it was nice to be able to talk to someone about something other than her political future.

"You know, I'm really going to miss you," she said sincerely.

"Then don't leave," Skye countered.

Kendra gave her a look and Skye finally softened.

"I'll miss you too, government girl. Promise me that you'll come back and visit when you can, okay?"

"I promise."

CHAPTER 10

Once her year in Aesira was over, Kendra had to admit that Skye was right – compared to Stanton, Aesira was boring. It might have been because of the vast farmlands that occupied most of the island, or it might have been because of Skye's absence, or it might have been a bit of both. Thankfully the lack of social activities wasn't a problem, as it gave Kendra time to organize all of the information she'd gathered during her time in Stanton. She'd even managed to visit Skye a few times and reassure her that her new roommate at Aesira University wasn't as fun.

When the summer arrived, Kendra headed to Cambria to take their summer defence course. After the Second Invasion, once Tecken was properly under the ISS's control, the Council assured everyone that there would be no more conflicts in the Segment. This meant that the Cambrian Forces, which had increased drastically ever since the First Invasion, had to trim down and widen their range. They still had a small contingent of soldiers, but now they offered training to the public, allowing anyone to sign up for classes on how to protect themselves and use their element.

Learning self-defence hadn't occurred to her until it had been suggested by Pitor. He was worried that once her true parentage was revealed, she'd become a target, and he wanted her to have some kind of knowledge of how to defend herself. It was a smart decision – especially considering that her next stop was Briton University. Living on Stanton had been difficult because it brought up a lot of memories and feelings, but living on Briton would mean being surrounded by Humanists.

The Church of Humanity was the lynch pin for her plan, as it had been back when Magnus Erikson the First realized that the Council of Twelve wasn't looking out for anyone's well-being but their own. The Council had managed to stop wars, but they had no idea how to stop hatred. Under their peace-loving eyes, the Church had been allowed to grow and spread their teachings, and now they were too large to stop. Everything Kendra knew about them was second-hand information, but none of it was good. As much as she'd prefer not to spend eight months on Briton, she needed to do this.

Dying her hair to a more Humanist colour was a small change, but it was important. Her hair would be her costume – helping her get into character. Every time she looked in the mirror, she'd see the strands of black hair and remember her purpose.

The decision to do this had seemed like a no-brainer, but in fact she'd had numerous discussions with Pitor about it. Kendra could tell that he wanted her to dye her hair, and she was more than ready to agree, but before he accepted her decision, he pushed her to justify why it would be best. Although it would be beneficial to keep her natural hair colour and experience the hatred of the Humanists first hand, she knew that she'd learn more about how they operated if they thought she was one of them. The idea of pretending to be a Humanist was sickening, but she needed to know what they were truly like. If she had personal knowledge of how they operated, then it would be easier to stop them.

She'd be walking a fine line while on Briton – pretending to be on the Humanists' side enough to get them to show their true colours around her, while not actually causing harm or distress to any Elementals. It would be difficult, but it had to be done.

Δ

When Kendra first arrived on Briton she noticed that the island seemed like every other, with the same green parks, the same blue sky, and the same ISS building standing tall in the centre of the island. There were differences, but they were subtle. The people who walked the street mostly had hair colours approved by Humanists – dark yellow, brown, black, and grey. She could walk for minutes without seeing a single 'un-natural' hair colour. Most of the clothing was also subdued, with very few people wearing bright tones.

After the Second Invasion, the Centre finally turned its eye toward the hatred and discrimination happening on Briton, stationing people on the island to ensure that peace was being maintained. Around that time, the Humanists started keeping a low profile, and stories about their wrongdoings halted. In the years since, the pressure on Humanists had lessened, but reports from the ISS stated that all was still well. The reports were so positive that Kendra had wondered if she'd arrive on Briton to find no proof to help her cause.

However, the truth of the situation was all around her. All anyone had to do was open their eyes and see for themselves.

CHAPTER 11

Her roommate was already unpacking when Kendra arrived at the dorm. She gave Kendra a bright smile, and went straight over to her, extending her hand.

"Hi, I'm Sara Johnson," she said. "I guess we're going to be roommate this year."

"Kendra Chen," she replied, shaking Sara's hand. It was obvious that Sara was a Humanist, from her brown hair and green eyes right down to her Biblically-Humanist name.

"Is this your first year?" Sara asked.

"It's my fourth, actually. You?"

"It's my third. I spent the first two years living at home, but then I figured that I should get the whole 'being independent' experience at some point," she smiled.

She was nice, and Kendra wondered if she was a Humanist because of her parents or if she was a true believer.

"That's why I decided to travel to different universities," Kendra said, returning the smile. "Might as well see the rest of the Segment before I settle down."

"So, if this is your fourth year, you must be turning twenty-one soon…"

The question was meant to be harmless, but Kendra recognized the meaning behind it.

She nodded, keeping the smile on her face. "I turned twenty last month," she lied, "so there's still plenty of time for me to figure it out."

The statement was deliberately left open to interpretation, and her roommate took the bait.

"Not sure if you want to Accept?" she asked compassionately.

Kendra shrugged. "Honestly, the whole thing is a lot more complicated than everyone thinks. I mean, lots of people assume that we're supposed to Accept, but if that were the case, it wouldn't be a choice, right?"

Sara nodded. "Is that why you decided to study here? To get away from all that 'We're Elementals so we have to Accept' propaganda?"

"Well, I just wanted to make sure that I understood all of my options. I mean, people say that it's what we're supposed to do, but if the Six-Elemental hadn't Accepted her powers, then the Second Invasion wouldn't have happened, and all those people wouldn't have died. Right?"

Sara paused to think, and Kendra wondered if she had laid it on too thick. Thankfully, Sara said the exact thing she'd been hoping to hear.

"Have you ever been to the Church of Humanity?"

Δ

The Church had services every day, but Sara informed her that the weekends were the best time to attend, especially for busy students. She used to attend the church near her parent's home, but now that she was living on campus, the location on 8th Avenue was closer. One of the advantages of the Church of Humanity was that it seemed to have locations on every block.

"I have a present for you!" Sara said, holding out a book. It was Saturday, the day before Kendra's first service.

Kendra took the book, noticing that it was a copy of the Humanist Bible. It was worn and well-used, obviously second-hand. Some of the page corners had been turned down, and the spine was cracked in a few places.

"It's an old copy of mine," Sara explained. "My parents gave me a new one when I decided to move out, and I'd like you to have this one. I hope you don't mind that it's used."

"Not at all. Thank you," Kendra said. "I really appreciate it."

It wasn't a lie. Having Sara's old bible would be a good insight into her mind and the minds of other Humanists. Before going to Briton, Pitor had Kendra read an old bible from Archaic Earth, before the Last World War, when Humans still existed and the Earth was filled with giant land masses called Continents. There weren't many copies of that book still intact, but Pitor had a habit of collecting rare publications. It had been much larger than the book she held right now, and she couldn't wait to see what had been left out and, more importantly, what had been left in.

That Sunday morning, as they walked up to the church, Kendra steadied her nerves and tried to act relaxed. She had no idea what to expect and was surprised by how friendly and welcoming the people were. Many of them smiled at her and greeted her kindly. She wondered if it was because she was new and they desperately wanted her to join them, or if they were genuinely nice. It was probably the first one. Kendra doubted that they would have been this kind if she'd shown up with her natural dark purple hair.

The building the service was in had probably started out small and modest, but over time there had been additions made and adornments added. The new clashed with the old, with bright shiny crosses hanging on faded wallpaper, and polished wooden pews standing on a worn floor. Kendra wondered if there was some symbolic reason for it, like if they were honouring the old while celebrating the new, or if they simply didn't care about some things as much as others.

She followed Sara into one of the pews, her roommate smiling brightly with anticipation, and as they sat down, Kendra prepared herself for what was to come.

After the service was over, she was almost disappointed. The sermons seemed harmless, with the preacher reading passages from the Humanist Bible instead of spouting vitriol about Elementals. There were parables and teachings, but no fire or brimstone. She had expected more from them.

It was only after a few more services that Kendra began to pick up on the subtleties. The preacher only ever used the word 'Human' and never 'Elemental'. There were sermons about how God should be the only all-powerful being in the world, worshipping other Gods was evil, temptation existed for us to prove our strength, and we should always strive to humble ourselves in God's eyes. There was never anything directly said about the evils of Accepting or having an element, but it always seemed to be implied. Kendra wondered if they had secret sermons for the true believers, where the gloves came off and they were allowed to share their true feelings.

Those messages were spread throughout the Humanist Bible. Although she couldn't remember everything that had been in the Archaic Earth bible, Kendra had a feeling that many of the stories had been modified to suit the Humanists' agenda. Stories that were originally about rich versus poor had been changed to powerful versus weak, and parables about being a good servant always involved saying no to any kind of power that might be offered to you. She also doubted that the original bible had used the word 'deny' so many times, as it had not been such a significant word before Elementals existed.

Many of the pages that Sara had marked involved stories about being kind and honest, but there were also numerous passages about denying. It might have been her subtle way of convincing Kendra to Deny, or perhaps she had been trying to convince herself that this was the best way. Sara wasn't as zealous as other church-goers, which made Kendra wonder again if she was a Humanist because it was something she truly believed in or if someone else had convinced her that this was the only way. Life on this island couldn't be easy for non-believers.

The more time Kendra spent on Briton, the more she saw how the Church's teachings influenced even the smallest action. Anyone with a different hair or eye colour was given long, discouraging looks. In stores and restaurants they were made to wait longer or were given brisk, unpleasant service, or sometimes their every action was followed, as if the person watching suspected them of wrongdoing. Elementals were made to feel as if there was something wrong with them – as if they were outsiders. The worst part was that there wasn't anything any of them could do about it. They couldn't go up to the ISS and tell them that a teacher had treated them differently, because they couldn't prove it. What the Humanists were doing wasn't outright discrimination, but it was enough to make a person feel uncomfortable and unwanted.

Kendra could understand why many Elementals didn't want to live here – it was much easier to move to another island where they wouldn't have to put up with this kind of treatment. Because of this, the Elemental population on Briton decreased and the Humanist population grew. If something wasn't done about it, within a few decades the island would be populated only by Humanists.

Δ

Sara was delighted that Kendra continued to regularly attend the church. Although Kendra maintained her indecision and never said anything definite about becoming a Humanist, she seemed to have won her roommate's trust. In the beginning Sara used to hover a lot more, finding excuses to be in their shared room whenever Kendra was there, as if she was afraid that leaving Kendra on her own would result in her Accepting. After a couple months, though, she spent more time away, leaving Kendra to her own devices.

Once she learned how much Kendra liked to read, she recommended a few bookstores that Kendra would have to visit before the school year was over. It turned out that there were a lot of little shops hidden throughout the island, most of which didn't have signs and didn't look like businesses from the outside. Kendra had walked past a few of them many times, barely giving them a second look because they appeared to be normal houses. It seemed that the only way to know what they really were was to have a Humanist tell you, which meant that they had to trust you.

Despite this, the employees of these stores looked at newcomers warily. On her first visit to one of the bookstores, Kendra noticed the suspicion in the cashier's eyes, so she greeted him with a friendly smile and mentioned that her roommate had recommended this store – being sure to use Sara's first and last name. After that, he'd warmed up considerably. A few more visits, a few discussions about the latest church service, and he was greeting her as if she'd been shopping there forever.

These bookstores were filled with books that Kendra had never heard of and were likely only published on Briton. There were essays about the virtues of Denying elements, biographical stories about people who had found peace through joining the Church of Humanity, and many fictional stories about how Elementals were going to destroy the world. There was even a secret collection that she was allowed to borrow from but couldn't purchase, which contained stories filled with hatred and prejudice towards anyone who Accepted.

Kendra loved to read, but most of these books were hard to get through. Although there was one topic in particular that she couldn't completely disagree with – the dangerous nature of the Six-Elemental. It felt wrong to agree with Humanists on any matter, but at least her hatred was born of knowledge and facts. She believed that this kind of power would be helpful if it were in proper hands, while Humanists saw the failings of the current Six-Elemental as proof that power corrupted. A lot of the anti-Six-Elemental books carried underlying messages about how terrible Accepting an element was and how people couldn't be trusted with such power. Frequently they showed how bleak the future would be once they had all bowed down to the totalitarian command of an all-powerful being. No one seemed to notice the irony of how the Humanists' goal was to control everyone and take away any personal choices they had.

But books weren't the only resource that the Humanists had on hand – a much subtler weapon was the island's newspaper, the *Briton Truth*. The writers had the same technique as the churches – to only say 'human' and sound as 'normal' as possible. The crime reports always referred to suspects as having differently coloured hair or Elemental Tattoos. At one point, Kendra started to wonder if all these crimes were actually happening or if they were being fabricated to make Elementals look bad.

The psychology of this was tremendous. After constantly reading about crimes perpetrated by Elementals, Humanists would look at every Elemental suspiciously, and innocent Elementals would start to feel guilty by association. The police, who were mostly staffed by Humanists, would have excuses to stop anyone they liked for questioning or arrest anyone who might fit the profile.

Whenever an Elemental was attacked, there would soon be a report exonerating the attackers. These people were simply being vigilant, protecting their homes from a perceived threat. The reports would say that it was terrible that they made a mistake and attacked the wrong person, but their hearts were in the right place.

Frankly, it was astonishing how the Humanists managed to keep up their agenda while pretending to obey the new laws against hatred, but it helped that they occupied most of the positions of power on the island. There was no balance here, no objectivity, only hidden malice in everything they did. Kendra would have admired it if it wasn't so horrifying.

Δ

It was a warm, sunny afternoon as Kendra headed out to the bookstore. On other islands she would have admired the nice weather and beautiful scenery, but on Briton all she could see was how twisted everything was.

As she walked, she made sure to keep her eyes open. One of the reasons she preferred to shop at a bookstore that was further away from her dorm was because walking around Briton was a learning experience. Watching this island's everyday life provided her with plenty of examples of the Humanists' influence, so if she could help it, she walked everywhere instead of taking her Sol-car. Many times she'd watched as Humanists unconsciously sneered or glared whenever they saw someone with a non-Humanist hair colour, as if their hatred was so strong that it could not be contained.

Sure enough, barely fifteen minutes into her walk, she witnessed a group of three people accosting a young man with light purple hair. The three had surrounded him and it sounded as if they were accusing him of some kind of crime. The man was loudly proclaiming his innocence, but it was having no effect. If he tried to move away, they would block his path, shoving him and demanding that he confess. Kendra had no doubt that the man was innocent, but there was nothing she could do. As much as she wanted to go over and break up the incident, she needed to keep her head down. If she was declared an Elemental-sympathizer, all of the work she'd done up to now would be for nought.

As tough as it was to continue walking and pretend that she hadn't seen anything, she knew that it had to be done. For now, the only thing she could do was nothing, but she vowed that someday in the future, she would do what the Council could not and stop all of this.

CHAPTER 12

Her twenty-first birthday was a month and a half into the New Year, but nobody on Briton knew it. Although Kendra had worked hard not to lie to anyone on any of the other islands, she had broken that rule on Briton. She needed the Humanists to see her as a potential ally, which wouldn't happen if she let them assume anything about her. Pitor had told her that it was okay to lie to those on Briton, because she was there for a bigger purpose. The rest of the Segment needed to see her as someone they could look up to for guidance, but Humanists would eventually grow to fear her.

Having her birthday on Briton was the biggest risk she'd had to take so far. While there was always the possibility that she wouldn't get a vision, Kendra knew that if she was given a vision, she would Accept that power no matter what element it was. But it wasn't just the power that worried her, it was the mark of power that came with it. The Elemental Tattoo could show up anywhere on her body and if it was in a place that couldn't be hidden, such as her neck or hands, then her secret would be discovered and her cover blown. Hopefully luck would be on her side.

The day before her actual birthday, Kendra pretended to come down with the flu. It carried over to the next day, giving her a perfectly reasonable excuse to stay in bed and miss class, as well as an explanation in case she happened to zone out during a conversation. Sara was none the wiser, wishing her well and offering to bring some soup later that day before leaving for class.

Kendra was in the middle of a book about a group of Humanists who had banded together to take down the Six-Elemental when her vision came. Everything went black and suddenly she saw a giant fireball before her, burning brightly with orange, yellow, and red flames flickering all over it. The fireball crashed into the side of a mountain, both objects exploding outward with tremendous force. Then everything went black and her mind cleared. There was no doubt in her mind when she thought, "Yes".

After her sight came back, she held her breath and waited. A few seconds later she felt the tell-tale prickling of the Tattoo that accompanied her element, in the very centre of her back. The breath she let out was more like a sigh of relief. That part of her body wasn't usually seen by anyone else – she'd be able to keep this secret easily.

Although she felt the urge to immediately start practicing with her element, she knew that it would have to wait. In only a few months she'd be off this island and able to practice freely.

CHAPTER 13

As soon as Kendra arrived on Cambria, she felt a tension she didn't know she'd been holding start to melt away. A highway was all that separated Cambria from Briton, but the islands might as well have been on opposite ends of the planet. Spending two semesters on Briton had seemed like a short task, but those eight months had felt like years.

Although she only had to spend three months on the island as an Elemental, she was constantly worried that she would be found out. It wouldn't have surprised her if Humanists had somehow learned to smell Elementals or sense their presence. Luckily her vigilance paid off and nobody discovered her secret. She left the island, telling Sara that she was going to go back home with all the knowledge she'd discovered. When Sara asked if she'd made up her mind regarding Acceptance, Kendra smiled and said that she had a lot of information to sift through, but implied that she was leaning towards Denying and made sure that Sara knew she was taking the bible with her. The look on Sara's face was almost one of relief, and Kendra wouldn't have been surprised if someone else was putting pressure on her to get her to become one of them.

By the end of her time on the island, Kendra could understand why Briton was so dangerous. The Humanists wanted the

The Fifth Queen

island all to themselves, and without any Elementals there to challenge them they would become a hateful vacuum, spreading their prejudice unopposed. How long would it be until the Humanists tired of only having one island under their control and tried to spread out to other islands? How long until the entire Segment was unsafe for Elementals?

Briton was a warning sign for what could happen when those in power turned a blind eye to obvious hatred, and she now understood why the Eriksons had put such emphasis on this island when they talked about creating a better world. The Council thought they had everything under control, but they'd only put a bandage over a deep cut. Laws were good and all, but if you couldn't prove that someone had broken one of them, or if the people enforcing the rules were just as corrupt as those breaking them, then you'd never achieve any success.

If her time on Briton was any indication, after sixteen years of being quiet, the Humanists were starting to fall back into their old, hateful ways. Before long, they'd be back to full power, being openly hateful and intolerant to all Elementals.

The more Kendra learned about history, the more surprised she was at how often it repeated itself.

Δ

The first day of training was just as tough as she remembered. By the time classes finished, almost every muscle ached. When Kendra looked over at her roommate, Xan, she noticed that he looked worse than she felt. Xan was taking the same elemental training course, so they were in the same classes, but it was his first year, so he had no idea what he was in for. Those going into elemental training knew that they'd first have to complete a week of basic training, but most didn't realize it would be so intense. The Cambrian motto was to train the body as well as the mind, so if anyone wanted to learn how to use their element, they'd first have to survive basic training. Kendra wondered if this was the reason some people didn't bother taking the course and if it wasn't counter-productive to the new Forces mandate.

"Want. To. Die," Xan said as they walked out of the training room.

"Showers first," Kendra replied. "The hotter the better. And stretch out those muscles while you're in there. Trust me."

It was something she'd learned during her previous course, that a hot shower after training helped relieve some of the pain in her aching muscles. Considering how much the two of them were sweating after running all those drills, showering was also a very practical idea.

As the hot water soothed her muscles, Kendra realized that she'd been optimistic to think that the second time around would be easier. Maybe that would've been the case if she'd trained every day in between, but other than jogging every day or so, Kendra had done nothing. She'd been too busy concentrating on her studies and trying to infiltrate the Humanists. Hopefully her muscles would realize that all of this was familiar and stop aching soon.

When she was finished, she waited for Xan outside the shower room. He emerged ten minutes later, looking much better than when he'd gone in.

"Okay, that helped. Good advice, Chen," he said.

"I've already told you to call me Kendra," she replied, smiling. "And I'm glad I could help."

They walked back to their room, commiserating about how out of shape they both felt. Lia and Will, their other roommates, were already in the room, having finished their last class an hour earlier. Lia and Will were both from Cambria, although they hadn't talked to each other before becoming roommates.

Xan was from Aesira, so Kendra was able to imply that she was from Drakkar.

"It's unfair," Xan said, collapsing onto his bed. "All I want is to learn how to set things on fire with my mind... Why do I have to run and jump so much?"

"I take it you two had a fun first day?" Lia smirked.

"The price to pay for having an element," Xan sighed.

"That's almost enough to make me not want an element." She paused. "Almost."

"Well, if you want to come back once you've Accepted," Kendra said, "I suggest you keep training in between. That class kicked my butt."

Lia nodded. "I shall keep that in mind."

Kendra liked her new roommates. Last year her roommates had all been in different courses and they'd spent most of their time apart, making friends with people in their classes. This year Kendra was in the same class as Xan, and Will and Lia were taking the introductory basic training class. Lia was only twenty, but Will was twenty-one and was an air elemental. Despite this, he had no desire to take the elemental training course – something the others couldn't understand.

"But why wouldn't you do the Elemental training?" Lia had asked him upon learning this.

"I'd rather just learn the general stuff," he'd replied.

"But they've got mixed classes, so you can do both at the same time."

"Yeah," Xan chimed in. "Don't you want to learn how to be cool and knock stuff over and push people around?"

Will raised an eyebrow. "Are you here to learn how to set people on fire?"

"Of course not! I mostly want to start campfires and heat up cold tea."

"I can't wait until my birthday," Lia said dreamily. "I hope I get a really cool element, like ice or electricity."

"Why don't you care about training with your element?" Kendra asked Will.

"Air is stupid," he huffed. "It's not the element I wanted, so why should I waste my time learning how to use it. All I could do is mildly annoy people."

Xan sighed melodramatically. "Yeah, air *totally* isn't as cool an element as fire. If I had air, I *definitely* wouldn't bother training. I'd just throw myself off the first bridge I saw – *that's* how lame air is."

Will tried to glare at him but ended up laughing in spite of himself. Xan and Lia joined in.

"You know, the Six-Elemental killed Magnus Erikson with air."

Everyone turned to Kendra.

"What did you say?" Lia asked.

"She suffocated him," Kendra helpfully elaborated. "Drove all the air away from him so he couldn't breathe."

"But I thought the cause of death wasn't released," Lia said.

"Wait," Xan remarked, straightening up. "Wasn't there something about how the Six-Elemental killed Erikson without leaving a mark on him? Suffocation would totally make sense."

Kendra shrugged. "It's an urban legend I heard once. I don't know if it's true, but if it is, it proves that air might not be the lamest element." She looked accusingly at Will.

"I wonder how long someone would have to train to be able to do that..." Xan muttered to himself, getting lost in his own thoughts.

"Good effort, Kendra," Will said, "but it's going to take

more than an urban legend to get me to think air's cool – especially since I don't need to kill any megalomaniac leaders. Why couldn't I have gotten electricity instead?"

Although Kendra couldn't understand why someone would Accept a power that they had no interest in, she'd decided to leave good enough alone. It sounded like Will wasn't going to change his mind any time soon, so anything she said on the matter would be wasted breath.

If anything, the exhaustion felt by Xan and her after their first class was confirmation to Will that his decision had been the right one.

"You mocked me, but I bet you're both wishing you hadn't chosen elemental training," Will smirked, stretching out his not-so-sore muscles. "Right?"

Xan shot him an unimpressed look from where he was still lying on his bed, using the least amount of effort possible. "Just you wait, Will. In a few weeks I'm going to set fire to your socks."

Δ

The next week they moved onto elemental training, which meant that Kendra was finally going to learn how to use her power. It had been too risky to try using an element on Briton, especially one as dangerous as fire, so she hadn't had a chance to try it out yet. She told herself that it was a good thing she was going into training fresh, as there were no bad habits to unlearn.

Their class split off according to their elements, leaving only six people in the fire course. The instructor focused on controlling fire instead of using it as a weapon, but Kendra knew that the lessons would still be beneficial. After all, learning how to contain a fire and shrink it down was simply the opposite of learning how to increase it. It was too dangerous to try applying that kind of knowledge here, but once she was away from the base, she'd be able to put it to the test. Of course, first she'd need to find a safe place to practice.

"Wow, you're really into this," Xan said after one of their classes. "You were intensely focused."

"Did I forget to mention that I really like fire?" she teased.

"At least I know that if I ever need help, I can ask you."

"In that case, I promise not to take it easy on you."

She knew that Xan had no real plans to use his element, but was glad that he was taking the time to learn how to control it, unlike Will. If Will ever found himself in a situation where his element would be helpful, he'd regret his decision – especially if someone ended up hurt because of that inexperience.

On Tecken, before the ISS took control, participation in the army had been mandatory. Each person, once they'd graduated, went into two years of training, learning how to fight and protect themselves, and eventually learning how to control their element – if they Accepted one. The Eriksons knew how important it was that every person on the island be able to control themselves and their power, but the ISS didn't seem to care.

Theoretically, it sounded like a good idea to have mandatory classes for all Elementals, but in this day and age there would have to be some discretion. There were many people who Accepted in secret – especially on Briton – who wouldn't want anyone to find out the truth. Then again, once Kendra managed to rid the Segment of prejudice, maybe there would be no more need for secrets.

As she lay in bed that night, she thought about the kind of world she wished everyone could live in – a world free of hatred. It wouldn't be easy to create this utopia. The days of declaring oneself an Erikson and demanding your rightful place in power were over.

Before her high school graduation, Pitor and she had mapped out exactly how she would rise to power. Once she had finished all of her practical learning on the other islands, she would return to Tecken and work for the ISS, growing through the ranks until eventually taking over as Leader. From there she would follow the path of Magnus Erikson the First, becoming beloved by all before turning her charm to the rest of the Segment.

That had been the plan, but over the years it started to look too simplistic. As Kendra travelled through the Segment and learned more about the people and politics, she began to think differently. The problems plaguing the Segment weren't as simple as she'd thought and solving them would require more than marching onto an island with an army and telling everyone to surrender. The more she learned, the more she realized that this wouldn't work. After all, she knew how both Magnus Erikson's plans had played out – domination, war, death, and failure. If she followed their path, eventually she'd end up the same. There had be another way: a better way.

She hadn't mentioned any of these thoughts to Pitor because she knew he wouldn't understand. He would try to keep her on the same course, but she couldn't do it any longer. Pitor had never been off of Tecken, so he didn't understand what it was like to live in a different place, with a different history, with your own concerns and issues. The people of the Segment would need a reason to follow her, and she intended to give them a good one.

Over the past few years, a new plan had formed in Kendra's mind, one that considered all the mistakes of the past and worked out how to avoid them – a plan that didn't involve making the same mistakes over again. A plan that would surely result in success.

But even with this new path, there was still one thing standing in her way. Pitor had told her not to concern herself with the Six-Elemental, but the more Kendra learned, the more she began to realize how much of a threat Tyler was. As long as the Heroic Six-Elemental was around, Kendra's dream would always be in danger of failing.

If she wanted to succeed, something would have to be done.

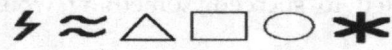

PART
TWO

CHAPTER 14
FIVE MONTHS LATER. STANTON

Kit Tyler woke up in a cold sweat, bedsheets tangled around her body. The details of her nightmare were slipping away, but the sense of fear and desperation it had brought remained. Breathing hard, she put her hand on her heart and reassured herself that it was just a dream. She was in her apartment on Stanton, she was surrounded by friends, and she knew who she truly was. She was safe. Repeating the words over and over, Kit felt herself calming down with each reprise. She was in her apartment on Stanton, she was surrounded by friends, and she knew who she truly was. She was safe.

The nightmares came less frequently these days, and sometimes she could go months without having one, but then something would trigger her and they'd start up again. She'd hoped that over time her memories of all the terrible things she'd done while brainwashed by the Tecken army would fade, but whenever they came back they were just as strong as they'd been sixteen years ago.

Eventually her breathing steadied and her heart stopped racing. After calming down, she noticed that she was alone in the bed. A glance at the clock showed that it was almost six in the morning. Untangling herself from the sheets, she headed to the living room, walking softly.

When she entered the room, she saw that Vaughn was sitting on the couch, reading. He was still wearing his night clothes and his red hair was sticking out in a few places. There would only be one reason he'd be awake this early, and it wasn't good.

"I did it again," she said, her voice filled with regret.

He put down the book and took a deep breath. When he turned to face her, it looked like he was going to say no, but then he paused and nodded.

"Yeah," he admitted.

Her heart sank. She would take ten times as many nightmares if it meant that she'd never call out Nathan's name again. Any person would be disheartened to hear their partner call out a former lover's name in their sleep, but Vaughn's loathing for Nathan went beyond simple jealousy. Not even Nathan's death had been enough to cure Vaughn of his intense hatred for the man.

It used to happen more frequently after the Second Invasion, when the memories were still fresh in her mind. At first Vaughn tried to hide what was happening, but eventually Kit caught on that something wasn't right, and he'd confessed. The realization had horrified her, and she hated that she was doing something that caused him pain, even if it was something that she had no idea how to stop. The incidents had lessened over time, sometimes not occurring for months, but every now and then she'd wake up to find Vaughn sleeping on the couch.

"What did I say?" she asked.

"I don't want to get into specifics, but it was... You were happy."

"I am so sorry."

"You don't have to apologize. It's not your fault."

She gave him an unconvinced look.

He stood up and walked over to her. "I know that you

can't help it, so you should never feel guilty. And in the grand scheme of things, I shouldn't be bothered by it. Too many years have passed for me to still be so angry."

"I just wish I knew how to stop it once and for all," she said softly, her blue eyes turning down to the floor.

"Don't worry about it. It's a small price to pay to have you here with me." He hugged her, and she leaned into him, wrapping her arms around his waist. She closed her eyes and breathed in his scent, relieved to still have him here. There was a part of her that was constantly worried she'd wake up one morning and find out he'd gone – that she'd finally do something terrible enough for him to realize she wasn't worth the trouble.

"Have you been up long?" she asked.

"Only about an hour. I tried to sleep, but couldn't, so I started reading."

"Have you eaten yet?"

He shook his head.

"How do pancakes sound?" she asked, looking up into his white eyes and smiling.

He mirrored her smile. "Pancakes sound great."

4

Two people exited the gallery, stepping out into the dark, clear night. It was just after midnight and downtown Stanton was almost empty, with only a handful of people walking along the sidewalk. Most of the stores had closed hours ago, dimming their signs so that they stood dark and quiet along the street. The moon shone brightly in the night sky, surrounded by hundreds of twinkling stars.

Kit walked closer to the gallery, checking to see how many people were still inside, but there was only one person, pulling down the shade on one of the front windows. When she knocked on the door, the red-haired man turned to see who it was. At the sight of her, he broke into a smile.

"Evening," Vaughn greeted her, opening the door to let her inside. "You're just in time."

"If it's one thing I have, it's impeccable timing," she joked. "Was the crowd good tonight?"

He nodded and brought down the remaining shades, effectively shutting out the outside world. "It was great. Enough people to feel crowded, but not so many that you couldn't see the art. There were only a handful of people who wandered in, looking for something that wasn't artwork, and that was only during the first couple of hours. Maybe you could start attending these things before midnight."

She shook her head. "I'm sure if I returned, all of the celebrity-seekers would return as well, and I don't want to overshadow your work."

"I wouldn't mind a crowded exhibit. Besides, maybe they'd come in here looking for you and end up finding something they liked."

"Which is why it's better that I'm not here to distract them..."

Vaughn sighed, but before he could say anything, she quickly switched gears.

"Besides, I like having you to myself," she said, smiling playfully. "If I went to the regular party, I'd miss out on these private midnight tours."

"Ah," he said, returning her smile. "That's true."

She kissed him and slid her arm around his back. He placed an arm around her shoulders and the two of them moved through the gallery, taking time to stop and look at each piece of art.

The exhibit included two other artists, one who worked in watercolours and one who worked with clay, so they wandered through those pieces first, saving Vaughn's work for last. The watercolours were of gardens and nature, with the colours blending into each other, creating a dreamlike state that was almost serene. The clay pieces were all meant to be functional dishes, but there were angles and shapes to them that Kit found off-putting. She could see how they'd be considered works of art, but she'd rather look at them instead of think about using them.

When they moved on to Vaughn's photos, she couldn't help smiling. There were eight large pictures, all night scenes, with bursts of white light in each of them. The backgrounds were shades of blues, ranging from light blues around the edges of the white light, blending into a blue so dark that it was almost black. These shades highlighted the different shapes and forms in the picture, somehow making them both easy and difficult to pick out.

"Nice colour scheme," she teased.

"What can I say? I like blue." He gave her shoulders a squeeze and kissed the top of her head.

As she began to examine the pictures, he stayed silent, letting her form her own opinion about each piece.

She looked carefully at all of the pictures, being sure to give each one proper attention. The first was a shot of Main Street, with all the empty and dark stores contrasted by the bright street-lamps in front of them. The next was a large split-level house, with bright light coming from both the large picture window and a small window in the top left corner; this was followed by the ISS building standing tall in the centre of the picture, with streetlamps all around it; then a large warehouse which took up almost all of the picture, with two lights on above the small door on the right; then another house, this time smaller, with the only light coming from the bottom left window. There was one picture of the park, with the light obscured by the tree branches and leaves, and another of Main Street, from a different angle.

While she loved all of his work, she fell in love with the last picture. It was less crowded than the others, with only the land and sky, and the water beyond, but on the left side there was a streetlamp, bursting with bright light. There was something calming about the vastness of the sea and sky, but the streetlamp grounded you and kept you from falling into the distance. She had no idea how Vaughn had created such a beautiful photo with such ordinary sights.

"So...?" he said after a while.

"This one." She pointed at the last photo.

"Not the one with the ISS building?" he teased.

She laughed. "The last one is definitely my favourite."

"I thought that might be the one. That's why I had them put a hold on it."

She turned to him, surprised. "What? Why?"

"Because although I try to avoid hanging my own artwork all over our apartment, I don't mind if it's something you like." He smiled at her. "Also, you couldn't see your face, but when you were looking at that photo you seemed at peace. It's a good look on you."

She didn't know how Vaughn managed to do it, but he could turn a day that started out so terribly into one of the best. If she could live the rest of her life in this moment, it would be a life well spent.

"They'll deliver it after the show's over," he said.

"Thank you," she replied quietly. "So, does this have a name?"

He paused dramatically. "Even in the Darkness."

She repeated the title in her head and her brain filled in the rest of the saying. "...There is light?"

"Exactly," he nodded.

She looked at the paintings again, seeing the brightness of the lights against the dark backgrounds. When the sun went down you would expect the world to be plunged into complete darkness, but there was still light to be found. There was still hope.

She smiled. "I love it."

CHAPTER 15

When Kit returned to work at Skyline Architects, after the mess of the Second Invasion had been cleaned up, she'd been prepared for the staring and whispering and strange looks. However, she'd expected it to end after a few days or weeks. She hadn't thought that sixteen years later people would still look at her differently.

It hadn't helped that there had been a large influx of customers, all wanting a glimpse of the mythical Six-Elemental instead of an actual quote. In an effort to weed out those who weren't serious about doing business, Kit was no longer allowed to meet with clients and had been moved into a private office, out of view from prying eyes. Luckily she didn't mind doing the more solitary work, but she missed being around the other employees. She couldn't go to worksites to check on a project's progress, or inspect finished buildings, or even go out for lunch with her coworkers, because there would always be people staring at her or coming up to her. Even now there was the occasional client who would come into the office, looking around for something that wasn't a design, and who had no intention of actually hiring them. It was a waste of the other employee's time, and Kit knew that they didn't appreciate it – no matter how hard she tried to keep her head down and act normal. It wouldn't have helped to change jobs – this kind of thing would happen no matter where she worked.

It was one of the many ways the world reminded her that she didn't fit in like she used to. After the Second Invasion, when she'd decided to try to live a normal life, apparently nobody else had gotten that memo. Any time she began to feel like her old self, it was only a matter of days before someone would say something and she'd be reminded of what she was and what she'd done.

A few days after the gallery opening, Kit stayed late at work to put the finishing touches on a design. The world had faded away while she worked, thinking of how this design would soon become a reality, and how this house would become someone's home. She'd used to dream about living in a home of her own design, but these days the design looked less like a small, cute house and more like a high-security castle. It was easier to design homes for other, normal people.

There was only one other person still in the office by the time she left, and he was too busy to notice her, so she slipped out into the street without saying goodbye. As she walked home, she noticed more than a few people staring at her and realized that she'd left her hat back at the office. She thought about going back for it, but realized she'd have to pass all those people again. It was better to keep moving forward and try not to think about it. Picking up the pace, she tried not to pay attention to the people who stopped and stared, but while she was waiting for a chance to cross the street, there was a soft tap on her right shoulder. Kit took a deep breath and turned around, wondering if she'd see a fan, a hater, or a Follower of Six.

Standing behind her, with a wide-eyed expression on her face, was a young woman with brown skin and dark purple hair. "I'm sorry to bother you," the woman said, "but are you...

you know... her?"

Kit wanted to sigh, but she stayed polite. "Her who?"

"The, you know, Six-Elemental?"

"Yeah, that's me," she said matter-of-factly.

The woman's grey eyes grew wider. "Wow. I mean, I heard all the stories, but to actually run into you... Will you be doing any speaking at the Church of Six? I used to go all the time back home, and I'd love to talk to you about what it's like to be... you know... you."

"Sorry," Kit said politely, "but I don't attend. I find it best to stay out of the way."

The woman raised an eyebrow, but her look quickly changed to apologetic. "Oh, um, well, I'm sorry to bother you. Have a great day!"

She smiled politely. "You too."

The woman waved at her and walked away. Kit turned back to the intersection, eager for an opportunity to cross. There was something about talking to a Follower of Six that made her skin itch, and she wanted to get as far away from this spot as quickly as possible. She used to get letters every week from the Church, inviting her to come and speak at one of their services, but she never responded or appeared. Eventually the letters reduced to once a month, as a simple reminder that they would welcome her with open arms if she ever wanted to attend. While the Church organizers were fine with giving her space, some of their followers didn't quite get it and often approached her on the street. It bothered her because she didn't want to be anyone's messiah or God. She only wanted to disappear into the background.

Still, as annoying as it was to be held in such reverence by the Followers of Six, it was better than having someone yell '*Murderer*!' at her. As if she needed to be reminded of the horrible things she'd done during the war – as if those memories didn't constantly haunt her, day in and day out. She never knew if those people were from Tecken and were upset about how she'd ended the war, or if they were from elsewhere in the Segment and upset about how she'd caused the war in the first place. In the long run, it didn't matter. It had been a couple years since the last time a stranger had yelled something like that at her, but Kit could see the looks some of the people gave her and knew that even if they didn't say it, they were thinking it.

The rest of her walk home was thankfully absent of further interactions. As soon as she made it through the front door of the apartment building she felt herself start to relax. The door was always locked and the only people who could get in were those who lived in the building, which was one of the reasons she'd accepted the ISS's offer for her to move in. While she'd enjoyed sharing a large house with her friends, she had quickly grown tired of looking out the front window and seeing people gathered outside, staring at the door, waiting for her to make an appearance.

The house had been an ISS asset, which they'd allowed Kit, Vaughn, and their friends to occupy in exchange for them agreeing to keep an eye out for Tecken soldiers or sympathizers who might reside on the island. They hadn't been friends before moving in – the only people who'd known each other before this were the twins, Zenyth and Naydir Hansen – and although everyone had grown close, possibly due to their proximity or maybe because of the nature of their work, the Second Invasion had changed things. Cale Parrile became more serious and subdued after the war and finally decided to move to Aesira to get away from it all. Although Bryanna Kavail stayed in Stanton for a while and maintained her upbeat attitude, she eventually moved back to her home island of Drakkar.

Kit had half-expected the twins to move back to Cambria, but instead they moved into the apartment building with her and Vaughn. At first, they'd shared an apartment on the same floor as Kit and Vaughn's apartment, but when Naydir's partner, Sav, moved in with him, Zenyth found herself another apartment on the same floor.

Sometimes Kit felt guilty about living in the building, as it had been built for visiting Leaders, Council members, and employees of the ISS, but then she remembered that she had ended the war and helped clean up most of the mess. Although she had no desire to work for the ISS, she'd earned a safe place to live and some peace and quiet.

When she walked into her third floor apartment, she could smell Vaughn's cooking. Walking past the dining room table, she noticed that five places had been set.

"I thought Zenyth had to work," she said.

Vaughn turned away from the sauce he was stirring. "Her shift was switched, so she called to let me know she could make it. How was work today?"

"Good. Finally finished that big project, so that's a relief. They'll start building soon."

"That's great. I've got things pretty much in hand for supper, but I have no clue what to serve for dessert."

"I'll think while I change," she smiled. He turned back to the sauce and she headed towards the bedroom.

"Oh," he called out. "There's some mail for you on the end-table."

"Thanks!" She detoured into the living room, seeing a stack of envelopes on the small end-table in front of the couch. She picked out three that had her name on them and started opening them as she walked. The first was a newsletter from Current Architecture, which she put aside to read later. The second was her monthly reminder from the Followers of Six about their daily services, which she promptly tossed in the garbage. The third envelope contained only one sheet of paper. It was blank, except for one line of text in the middle of the page, reading: *Everything you know is a lie.*

She looked at the paper carefully, trying to see if there was anything else that could explain what it might mean, but there were no other words. The name on the return address was W. Eon-Sun, a name that she didn't recognize and didn't sound familiar to her in the least. The address was merely Stanton, Segment Delta.

Tossing the letter in the garbage with the monthly reminder, Kit figured that it was some kind of prank. She had no idea what the person who'd sent it was trying to accomplish, but if they couldn't communicate that idea well enough, then it wasn't worth any more of her time.

4

"We've finally decided to get married!" Naydir said, taking hold of Sav's hand. The two of them shared a smile before turning back to the table.

"That's fantastic!" Kit cheered. "You two are so great together."

"It's about time," Vaughn added, smiling.

"You're telling me," Zenyth remarked. "I've been telling my brother to lock down Sav for the past five years."

The rest of the table laughed. Naydir's job with the police force had him running reports to the ISS on almost a daily basis, but it had been pure chance that the two of them met. Sav worked in the security department, but through a few unlucky breaks one day, he'd ended up having to spend a few hours acting as the assistant for the Leader of Stanton. When Naydir arrived at the office with the reports, the attraction was instantaneous. They talked for so long that Naydir forgot why he'd come to the office in the first place. After a few more carefully orchestrated meetings, there was no going back, and when they started officially dating, everyone couldn't help noticing how well they complimented each other.

Although Sav never had any trouble telling the twins apart, despite how alike they looked with their tawny skin, short black hair, and green eyes, after a few years of dating, Naydir let his hair grow a little longer, like Sav's wavy grey hair. Zenyth refused to do the same, and for the first time since Kit had known them, there was a contrast between the twins other than their personalities.

"Well, I wasn't going anywhere," Sav said, giving Naydir's hand a gentle squeeze. "I just had to make sure that I wouldn't have to legally marry Zenyth as well, because that would have been a much more complicated ceremony."

"Hey, just because you're dating my twin, it doesn't mean that I'd want to marry you," Zenyth said. "I mean, I like hanging out with you two, but I am completely fine on my own."

"It's going to be a small ceremony," Naydir said, changing the subject. "Our parents, hopefully you two..."

"Of course," Vaughn replied.

"We're hoping that Bryanna and Cale will be able to make it. And, of course, some of Sav's friends."

"And although the ceremony will be small, there will be lots of celebrating," Sav added, his orange eyes twinkling as he laughed.

Zenyth looked over at Kit. "So, are you two going to get married any time soon?"

The bluntness of the question took Kit aback. She should have been expecting Zenyth to say something like that, but Zenyth had learned some tact over the past decade and wasn't as blunt as she used to be. Kit knew that the question hadn't been intended to be hurtful, but the answer wasn't so simple.

"Umm..." Kit tried to think of the right thing to say.

Vaughn saved her by putting his arm around her shoulders and giving her a little squeeze. "Maybe someday we'll think about it, but there's no rush."

"Well, no offence to you two," Sav said, "but there's no way I'd want you pulling focus from our wedding. So, if you decide to get married, you'd better make it a long ways away."

The table laughed, and Kit was thankful to Sav for diffusing the awkward situation. Before they started dating, Naydir had been the one apologizing for all of Zenyth's frankness, but Sav had quickly learned how to deal with any awkward situation. They made a great team.

The subject changed, but Kit only half paid attention. She was still thinking about Zenyth's question and how it had been right for her to ask it. Kit and Vaughn had been together for sixteen years and she wanted to spend the rest of her life with him, but it wasn't that simple. She couldn't marry him, because she didn't know if she could do that to him. Life with her wasn't easy – for a multitude of reasons. She'd deceived him when they first met, lying about having more than one element; when he discovered her secret, she'd blackmailed him into keeping it; her secret had led to her disappearing on him for weeks, and when she finally resurfaced she had been brainwashed into someone else, someone who didn't remember him; she'd also had a relationship during that time, and couldn't stop calling that person's name out in her sleep. And then there was the whole being the legendary Six-Elemental thing...

She couldn't ask Vaughn to spend the rest of his life dealing with her problems. If he ever wanted to go, she wanted him to have an easy way out – a door to go through if it all became too much. Marrying him would be like locking him into this life. It would make it hurt so much more if he ever decided to leave.

CHAPTER 16

Zenyth made herself a cup of strong tea before going back to her desk. While she could see the purpose of this new directive from the ISS, she didn't understand why every single police officer had to read through all the newspapers in the Segment. It would have been more efficient to assign the task to one person or share the papers between officers, but she supposed that the ISS had a reason for doing it this way. Whether it was a good reason or not, she had to follow orders.

Still, going through six island papers and a Segment paper every single shift was a bit much. Things were quiet at the moment, so it wasn't like she could argue that they had better things to do, but that didn't make the work any less tedious. After the Second Invasion there had almost been more work than they could handle, rounding up Tecken soldiers, searching for trouble-makers, and making sure the island was secure. These days most of the crime they dealt with consisted of young kids causing mischief. Just a few days ago she had to writeup two teenagers who were vandalizing trees in the park with a small knife. They weren't even smart about it, doing it in the middle of the afternoon in broad daylight. In fact, they were so occupied with their task that Zenyth had been able to walk right up to them without them noticing. She'd cleared her throat, causing both of them to jump, and then she'd sighed with as much disdain as possible. After taking down their names, she told them to find better things to do and sent them on their way. Their files had a list of other such incidents, but they were all childish pranks, so she added her latest encounter and hoped that someday soon they'd grow up.

Zenyth knew that she should appreciate these quiet days, because it meant that society was calming down, but instead she felt restless. She needed some kind of new project to sink her teeth into – preferably something that didn't involve four hours of reading.

Sitting down at her desk, she side-eyed the newspaper on top. She had saved the *Briton Truth* for last, knowing that it would be the newspaper that would annoy her the most. Other papers reported facts, but Briton managed to skew everything in a Humanist slant. Taking a sip of her tea, she sighed and started to read. As usual there were thinly-disguised jabs at Elementals and praise for the Church of Humanity – exactly what she'd come to expect. When she reached the crime pages, however, she sat up a little straighter and paid more attention.

It had taken her four days to notice the pattern, but now that she had she couldn't un-see it. Every single crime report in the paper involved an Elemental – and never on the innocent side. Any act of vandalism or theft or mischief was always attributed to someone with a non-Humanist hair colour or eye colour, or someone with a noticeable elemental Tattoo. Although Zenyth had never been to Briton, she knew that this ratio didn't make sense. There had to be a vast amount of Humanists living on the island, so how was it that they never caused any trouble? Were reports being left out to make the Humanists appear infallible? Were reports being falsified to make the Elementals look worse? Or was it both?

"Lei," she called out. "Have you finished your papers yet?"

She looked across the room, to where Officer Else Lei was sitting at her desk. Lei looked up from the folder she had been writing in and turned to Zenyth.

"Yeah. Passed them on to Kyron half an hour ago. Why?"

"Notice anything weird about the Briton crime pages?"

Lei let out a breath as she thought back to what she'd read. "Well, they've got more crime than any other island. Their police force must be run off their feet."

"Did you notice how all the perpetrators are Elementals, and how not a single Humanist causes any trouble?"

Lei shook her head. "I mean, it would make sense for Humanists to lie low. They got the spotlight pretty bad after the Second Invasion, and with the hate laws now officially on the books, it wouldn't be smart for them to be causing trouble like they've done in the past."

For a second Zenyth wondered if she was reading too much into the crime reports. She didn't like Humanists, so it wasn't hard for her to find fault with them, and Lei had made some good points. Then again, something felt off. The Church of Humanity had done nothing after the Second Invasion, other than quieting down. They hadn't revised their ideals or apologized for past actions or made a comment about how maybe it was okay to be an Elemental after all. It was entirely possible that the only thing they'd changed was the volume of their hatred – turning it from maximum to minimum.

Maybe it was because she'd heard Kit's stories about growing up on Briton, but Zenyth doubted that the Humanists would simply roll over and play dead. It was more likely that they were lying low, hoping to go unnoticed while they continued their wicked ways.

She wasn't surprised that Lei hadn't thought too hard about the Briton crime reports. Heck, before this assignment, Zenyth hadn't given much thought to any island other than Stanton. When the ISS reports came out after the Second Invasion stating that Briton seemed to have calmed down, everyone had nodded in relief and moved on. But maybe that was exactly what the Humanists had wanted.

Zenyth checked the clock to see how long she had before her rounds. There was just enough time for her to start pulling together a report. A few years ago, she'd have gone straight to the Chief's office, but these days she knew that a well-thought-out report was the way to go.

Sometimes it was tough to be an adult.

≈

It was late when Zenyth arrived home from work. As soon as she was through the door, she kicked off her shoes and headed to the kitchen to get a beer. She'd spent the last hour of work going through Briton's newspapers and needed something to help turn her brain off.

Leaning against the counter, she noticed that the dishes were piling up. It wasn't an immediate problem, but the dirty dishes were starting to outnumber the clean. Eventually she'd run out of clean spoons and have to jump into action, but today wasn't that day.

Living alone had been an eye-opener. Although she'd had her own room many times, she'd never had a whole apartment to herself. It took just over a week for the mess to start reaching critical mass and for her to realize how tidy Naydir was and how often he'd picked up after her or cleaned up a little mess before it became a big one. She'd never realized how exhausting it was to keep things clean all the time. In a moment of weakness, she'd considered hiring her brother to come in once a week and keep things clean, but then thought better of it – mostly because she didn't want him to think that she couldn't handle living alone. Although Naydir and Sav had been dating for eight years, they'd only been living together for the past three. They probably would have moved in together sooner, but Naydir put off telling her that he wanted to live with Sav for so long that Zenyth eventually caught on and had to bring it up to him.

That determined stubbornness was what got her through the first year living alone. She didn't want to admit that she missed her brother, so whenever she found herself feeling lonely she'd turn the television on or go for a walk or look up groups to join. She'd played a lot of different sports during those months, most of which she'd never play again. A lot of time had been spent hanging out with Kit and Vaughn, who never said anything about her sudden and frequent appearances. Naturally she'd visited Naydir and Sav, but had been careful not to be there too often. At first living alone had been, well, lonely, but then she learned how much she liked being by herself. She'd always enjoyed having time to herself and being in her own apartment meant that she didn't have to deal with other people in the morning.

She also learned how to deal with untidiness, letting things go their natural way until the urge to clean hit her. Looking at the dishes, she didn't feel even the slightest impulse to clean, so she took her beer and wandered into the living room.

Her mind went back to the report. It wasn't enough that she'd spotted a problem with Briton's police reporting, she also needed to come up with some kind of way to address it. Why bother pointing it out if she couldn't figure out how to fix it? It wouldn't be enough to go down there and ask for every police report from the past year – they'd need some kind of way to infiltrate either the police station or newspaper, or both. Maybe they could plant spies.

At that thought, she felt the start of a smile. It brought her back to sixteen years ago, when she'd been recruited by the ISS to located Tecken sympathizers and spies. Hiring a bunch of civilians to go around looking for suspicious things didn't sound like the best idea, but the team had managed to do a pretty good job. They'd identified a Tecken soldier – mostly thanks to her – and even though Kit had gotten herself kidnapped and brainwashed, they'd managed to rescue her before too much damage could be done. It had been a strange, crazy time, but these days Zenyth found herself missing the sense of purpose it had given her.

Of course she never wanted another war, but the thought of going on a secret mission was exciting enough. Maybe she'd be sent to Briton to investigate. It would make sense, considering the work she'd done for the ISS. Then again, there was a very real possibility that nothing would happen. The Chief would read her report, think that she was making a fuss over nothing, and life would go on as usual. But even if nothing became of this, she wanted to know that she'd done all she could.

Falling onto the couch, she turned on the television and started flicking through the channels. After settling on a movie she'd already seen a few times before, she shut her mind off and tried to relax.

CHAPTER 17

The next day was Kit's bi-monthly meeting with Augusta Frederick, the Leader of Stanton. Or, as she had started referring to it as, her bi-monthly waste of time because she still didn't want to work for the ISS. It had been one of the concessions when Kit moved into the apartment building, and she'd considered it a small price to pay for personal safety. When they first started negotiations, the ISS wanted to have weekly meetings, while Kit didn't want to attend any. Eventually both sides settled on once every two weeks.

In the beginning she'd try to get out of these meetings by pretending to be ill or having to work, but Frederick would insist that another meeting be scheduled to make up for the one they missed. Eventually Kit learned that it was easier to give in. The one consolation was that she didn't have to travel far. The meetings took place in Frederick's office on the top floor of the ISS building, which was only a few blocks away from the apartment building.

The meetings were disguised as 'Segment Updates', with Frederick filling Kit in on how things were going on each of the islands. In the beginning they used to be more informative, with notices about rebuilding that still needed to be done or rumours of possible uprisings in Tecken and Briton, but as the years passed the Segment quieted down. Now they weren't much more than thinly disguised attempts to get Kit to join the ISS.

Today she was feeling especially terrible, as her dreams last night had been filled with confusion. For the past five days she'd been getting letters with cryptic messages like: *Everything is false; Don't trust anyone;* and *They're all lying to you.* Kit had no idea who this Eon-Sun person was, but the letters they were sending were really getting annoying. In the past she'd received letters from Sixers praising her and others who were angry with her, but never before had she received anything so strange. It was weird enough that she'd started saving the letters, hoping to find some kind of message hidden within. On her way to the meeting she wondered if she should mention the letters to Frederick, but wasn't sure what would it accomplish. Would the ISS be able to find some meaning that she couldn't? It was more likely that they'd offer to investigate, but only if she agreed to work for them.

As Kit walked up the six floors to Frederick's office, taking the steps two at a time, she tried to look on the other bright side of these meetings – they were a great source of exercise. When she reached the top floor, she took a second to slow her heart rate before leaving the stairwell.

Entering the room outside of Frederick's office, Kit said hello to Teya, Frederick's receptionist.

"How are you doing today?" Teya said warmly.

Kit smiled. "Pretty good, considering. How's work?"

"Well, Frederick's got me sorting through some files, so that'll be a fun task for the week ahead."

"I wish you the best of luck."

They chatted for a few more minutes before Teya buzzed Frederick to let her know that Kit was here. A reply came immediately, telling Teya to let Kit in.

"Wish me luck," Kit whispered before going through the door. Frederick's office had been designed to meet and greet guests, being larger than any other office in the building. It was almost half of the floor and was long enough to have glass windows on three sides. Kit recalled the first time she visited the ISS building, meeting with the coordinator for the civilian team, Triton Kolsovar, and how she'd enjoyed the view from his office on the fourth floor. The view from Frederick's office put that one to shame.

Frederick greeted her as she walked in, gesturing to the informal sitting area to the left. She looked much older than when Kit had first met her, with more grey in her black hair and more wrinkles around her orange eyes – all side effects of having a leadership position during a war. Kit walked over and took her usual seat, a comfortable stuffed chair upholstered in dark green, closest to the door. The sitting area had two chairs and a small couch, all in the same dark green, arranged around a small table.

"Tea?" Frederick asked.

"Yes, thank you," Kit replied.

Frederick walked over to her small kitchenette and poured two cups of tea, carrying them over to the sitting area. Kit took one of the cups and thanked her.

"Have you seen the newspaper today?" Frederick asked, launching straight into it the second she was seated.

Kit nodded. "They might have found a small island nearby that they can use for farming. Sounds like a good idea."

Frederick frowned. "Did you read the opinion page?"

"I stopped reading that a long time ago. Why?"

She stood up and walked over to her desk. "Well, there's a rather interesting anonymous piece in today's edition." She picked up the paper from her desk and walked over to hand it to Kit. "It's all about regulating Elementals and bringing in mandatory registration with proof of Acceptance."

Kit took the paper and skimmed the article. "Why would anyone want that? What purpose would that possibly serve?"

"It's because of you," Frederick said bluntly. "The writer argues that if this system had been in place decades ago, we would have known who you were and what you could do, and then the Second Invasion would never have happened, because you'd have been safely on our side."

Kit lowered the paper. "But Erikson had been preparing for an invasion for... *forever*. I was just..." she trailed off, unsure how to continue that sentence.

Frederick shrugged. "You have to admit that the writer has a point. If we had known about you, we would have been able to intimidate Erikson into backing off."

"But you don't know that for sure. It might have put a giant target on my head. Erikson might have killed me and then invaded. There's no guarantee that it would have stopped him."

"I know, but you have to remember that we didn't tell the public everything that happened during the Second Invasion. Some people have formed their own opinions from the facts that were released, and some of those have been slightly misguided." She took a sip of tea. "And it's not like we're actually planning on implementing this kind of thing. It would be much too difficult to regulate."

"So why is the paper printing this kind of thing?" Kit found herself growing annoyed at the piece and whoever it was that had written it. It was a terrible thing to think – forcing people to out themselves as Elementals. She hated to think of what it would be like to live on Briton if this was ever enforced.

"We won't suppress anyone's ideas, as long as they don't

incite hate."

"But the idea of registration—"

"Kit," Frederick interrupted, "it's not really about registration. It's about you. The point of the piece isn't about the danger of Elementals, it's about the danger of the Six-Elemental existing without anyone's knowledge. It's about that power being put into the hands of someone who could abuse it." She took another drink. "Honestly, it's an old argument at this stage. I'm not sure why it's being brought up again, other than the fact that some people have nothing original to talk about."

"So, if it's an old argument, why are you telling me about it?"

"Because it's about you. You should keep up on that kind of thing, so that if anyone ever mentions it to you, you'll know what they're talking about, and be able to defend yourself."

"Defend myself? Do you think it'll come to that?"

Frederick shrugged again. "Let's hope not."

ﻪ

The meeting didn't last very long after that. It had fallen into the usual format after the strange beginning, with Frederick reminding Kit that there was still a place for her within the ISS. There was a new angle to the question this time, with an allusion to the fact that if Kit worked for them, they'd be able to handle any controversy around her, such as the opinion piece. As wonderful as it would be to not have to defend herself, she didn't like that the ISS was resorting to bribery.

On her way into her apartment, she checked the mail, finding another letter from W. Eon-Sun. Shoving the letter into her pocket, she sighed. The logical part of her brain told her to throw it straight into the garbage, but the part of her that was annoyed by the mystery of it all was hoping that this letter would finally be the one that explained what the point of all this was.

Vaughn was in the living room, cleaning his camera, when she entered.

"How'd it go?" he asked, putting the camera down.

She leaned in the doorway. "Well, they asked me to join them again, as usual, so they're staying consistent." Then she recounted the information about the opinion piece. She didn't bother mentioning the offer from the ISS to handle the media because she didn't want him thinking that she should take it.

"Oh, yeah. I read that piece this morning," he said.

"Why didn't you tell me?"

"Because it's nothing that you haven't heard before. And the ISS wouldn't let that kind of thing happen – it'd be a total invasion of privacy."

Kit thought back to when Vaughn first told her about his dishonourable discharge from the Cambrian Forces, and how it had been because he didn't want to tell anyone that he'd Accepted his element. If he had, the Forces would have made him sign up for elemental training, and he'd wanted to go into weapons training instead. The deception had worked for a while, but eventually he was found out. He'd taken a dishonourable discharge instead of staying and adhering to their rules. It was one of the things they had in common – they'd both lied about their elements.

She slumped on the couch next to him. "Frederick wants me to start reading the opinion pages so that I can be prepared if anyone brings it up."

"Why would anyone bring it up?"

She shrugged. "Apparently I'm back to being a hot topic. I wouldn't be surprised if reporters started calling again, asking my opinion on everything."

"Well, hopefully someone else will write into the papers, rebutting the opinion."

A laugh escaped her lips. "That would be pretty great. A bunch of people fighting through the opinion page, talking about something that they have no control over."

"Everyone needs some kind of hobby."

She sighed and stood up. "I need to change into more comfortable pants."

While she was changing out of her meeting clothes, she remembered the letter in her pocket. Before opening the envelope, she tried to guess what the paper might say this time. If it wasn't some kind of explanation, then it would probably be something stupid about not trusting herself or about the entire world being a lie. Maybe it would be a repeat of something she'd received before. There were only so many dumb ways a person could write about truth and lies.

When she opened the paper and read the words, her eyes widened and her breath caught in her throat. She looked around the room to make sure that she was alone, even though she knew that no one else was in there. As she looked at the letter again her mind raced back to the memory of a dark room and a tall person with white hair and white eyes. She was so tired, but the person wouldn't stop asking her the same question over and over – the same question written on the paper in front of her.

Where did you grow up?

Kit felt ill. Back when she was being held by Tecken soldiers, they'd tried to convince her that she'd grown up on Tecken and that her life on Briton and Stanton was a lie. They had asked her that very question over and over, waiting for her to give the answer they wanted. Whenever she said Briton, Wes, the person in charge of her reassignment, would explain why she was wrong and ask the question again. Kit had no idea how long she'd spent in that room, but it felt like years. She'd been so exhausted and confused, and eventually she didn't know what was real and what was fake.

That one sentence brought everything rushing back so fast that she had to sit down. All she could see was the image of Wes and her black and white tie with the swirls that seemed to move on their own. Kit quickly repeated the truth to herself – that she was born on Briton and lived in Stanton – and tried to force the memory away.

The person who wrote that letter had to know what that question meant, otherwise, why would they spend days building up to it with questions of not knowing what was real? It had to be some kind of game, but what was the purpose? What were they hoping to achieve? Kit took a careful look at the envelope, hoping that maybe she'd be able to find some kind of clue. The name still didn't ring any bells, but she noticed that the initials spelled out WES. Was it a coincidence or was Wes back, playing with her brain from a distance? Kit had told the ISS about the brainwashing, but they had been unable to find Wes anywhere on Tecken. Not only was she nowhere to be found, but there were no records of her ever existing. The ISS thought that Kit had hallucinated this person while under duress, but Kit knew that she was real.

Was Wes out there, somewhere, watching her? Seeking revenge for Kit breaking the reassignment and betraying Tecken? Was it possible that she had gone into hiding after the war, waiting for the right moment to resurface? But if that were the case, why now?

Kit took in a deep breath and tried to chase the questions away with her mantra. She was in her apartment on Stanton, she was surrounded by friends, and she knew who she truly was. She wouldn't let this get to her. She knew what the truth was.

ห

That night Kit dreamed that she was trapped in a dark room. There were no doors or windows, or any way for her to escape. There was some kind of light in the room, but she didn't know where it was coming from. It was just enough for her to make out the walls and herself, but nothing else. Suddenly the walls started to move, twisting themselves into spiral patterns that spun on their own accord. She tried to shut her eyes, but the spirals were still there, imprinted on the back of her eyelids.

Suddenly she heard Wes' voice calling her name, but when she opened her eyes there was no one else in the room.

Where did you grow up? Wes' voice asked, repeating the question over and over, growing louder each time until it was deafening.

When she finally woke up it felt like her ears were ringing. The room was dark and there was a moment of panic as she wondered if she was still inside the dream, but then she realized that the sun hadn't risen yet. This was her bedroom on Stanton, and she was safe. Vaughn was sleeping beside her, so at least she hadn't woken him up.

She sighed but didn't bother lying down again. There was no way she'd get back to sleep now, not after that dream. It was her own fault. She never should have opened the envelope – her stupid curiosity was going to be the death of her. At least now she knew why these letters were being sent to her, and she could ignore any more that arrived.

Her mind calmed and eventually she drifted off to sleep again, but her dreams were haunted by images of black and white spirals and questions about her past.

ห

Although Kit had managed to convince herself that she was done with all this letter nonsense, when she got home from work that day and saw another envelope waiting for her, she couldn't bring herself to leave it alone. She wanted to crumple it up and shove it in the garbage, but something was stopping her. What if there was more to it than she thought? What if there was a reason that this was happening now? Something that she couldn't see yet?

Ignoring the part of her that called her an idiot and a traitor, she ripped open the envelope and took out the letter. It read: *I need you to realize what's real and what's not.* This line helped confirm Kit's suspicions that Wes was behind it all, as this was another phrase that had been said many times during the reassignment.

Looking down at the letter, Kit heard the previous words echo in her mind. *Where did you grow up?* Was it possible that Wes was hoping that these letters would trigger something inside of her and make her think that she was with Tecken again? Was Wes trying to brainwash her through the mail? That couldn't be possible. A person couldn't be brainwashed by letters. Could they?

A cold shiver went up her spine.

CHAPTER 18

The envelopes didn't stop, but Kit could no longer bring herself to open them. She wanted to throw them away, but every time she stood over the garbage can she couldn't do it. What if they weren't garbage? What if they were important? What if they held a terrible secret that might come in handy some time in the future? Instead she hid them in her sock drawer with the other letters, tucking them all under a pile of socks in the back so that she wouldn't have to look at them. She was hoping that they'd be 'out of sight, out of mind', but whenever her gaze fell on the drawer, she could hear the letters calling out to her.

The smartest thing to do would be to tell Vaughn about the letters and have him throw out any more envelopes that arrived, but she couldn't do that. It was stupid that she'd let herself be so affected by words, and he'd probably be upset that she'd let it go on for so long. Maybe she could lie and say that they were from a Follower of Six, but he probably wouldn't understand why she was so wary of them. No, the best thing to do would be to continue hiding them away and hope that she never became curious enough to open them.

It managed to work until the next Sunday, when she noticed that the envelope was heavier than usual. The previous envelopes had been small, containing one sheet and one sentence, but this envelope definitely had more than one sheet of paper within. Although she knew that she should hide it away with the others, curiosity began to overwhelm her.

"Are you all right?" Vaughn asked her at supper. "You seem nervous."

"I'm fine," she said, smiling. She hoped that the smile looked natural and not forced.

"I could forgo my plans and stay home, if you'd like. It's supposed to be just as clear tomorrow night."

She shook her head. "It's just those stupid opinion pages that Frederick has me reading. I keep thinking that I see personal attacks in everything."

"Well, if they make you feel that way, maybe you should stop reading them."

It sounded so simple when he said it. And so relevant to what was actually going on.

"I'll get over it," she said. "Don't worry. You go out and take your fantastic photos, and I'll try not to let that kind of stuff bother me."

Her smile came easier this time, but she could see that he was still concerned.

"You know that you can talk to me about anything," he said. "Right?"

Her smile faltered. "I know, Vaughn."

He nodded to himself and finished eating. Kit tried to eat, but the conversation had ruined her appetite. She should tell Vaughn what was going on, but the words stuck in her throat.

After he left, she sat in their bedroom, looking at the envelope. She made a bargain with herself – if she opened this envelope, then she would tell Vaughn about everything that had been sent to her. However, if she put the envelope with the others and didn't look at it, then she could keep her secret, because there would be nothing to say.

Taking a deep breath, Kit opened the envelope.

The paper inside was yellowed with age, folded to fit inside the envelope. When she unfolded the stack of pages, she saw that the top paper was white and had one line typed on it: *It's time for you to learn the truth.*

A shiver went up her spine and she was struck with the feeling that she should put the pages away, that she had gone down this stupid path long enough, but for some reason she couldn't stop. Putting that page to the side, she looked at the yellowed pages underneath. There were five of them. Kit took a deep breath and started to read.

Report 4249. Sources have confirmed that the Council is behind the kidnapping of the Six-Elemental, A.K.A Katherine Tyler. They have moved her to Stanton for reassignment, but the location of their base is currently unknown. Our agents are trying to find the base and bring her back, but no results so far.

This event happened mere weeks after Tyler's twenty-first birthday, when she was revealed to be the Six-Elemental. Suspected Council spies have been detained, but we have yet to uncover the traitor behind this or learn how Tyler was removed from the island without our knowledge.

The search will continue.

End report.

She turned to the next page.

Report 4328. Sources have confirmed that the Six-Elemental is on Stanton. We are too late - she has been brainwashed into thinking that she is on the Council's side. In order to keep a close eye on her, she has been hired as part of a 'Civilian Team' for the ISS and surrounded by ISS employees.

Nathan Roane has made contact with Tyler and confirmed that she did not remember him. She appears to be completely on the Coun-

cil's side, although her Tecken beliefs have not been buried too deeply. We have assigned Roane to make further contact with her, as he is our best chance at bringing her back.

End report.

Her hand was shaking as she turned to the next page.

Report 4339. The rescue mission to bring Tyler back from the ISS was successful. She had to be taken by force as she was still deep under the Council's control, but we are confident that our operatives will be able to bring her mind back to us.

See attached report for more details.

She quickly moved to the next page, which was a medical report about her state of mind. It detailed how she couldn't remember anything about being born and raised on Tecken, and how she was absolutely convinced that she had been born on Briton.

Her breath caught in her throat. It was fake – it had to be. But why would someone write something like this? The pages could have been manipulated to look aged, but why would someone go to so much effort? Why try to trick her with such a blatant lie?

Hesitantly, she turned to the last page.

Report 4344. Tyler's mind has proved tougher than initially anticipated. Even Wes has admitted that this will be a harder job than she would like. We do not know what method the Council has used for their reassignment, but it has effectively erased Tyler's memory. Trying to call her real memories back will take much longer than originally thought, and that is if we are able to bring them back at all. Our only option at this point is to try to overwrite her current conditioning. There are no guarantees that this method will work, and many have raised their concerns that it may fail and she may turn against us, but we have no other choice. Hopefully being around all of her friends and colleagues will be enough to bring the truth back to her, and Tyler will be on our side, where she belongs.

End report.

The page fell from her hands, fluttering onto the floor. She couldn't believe what she'd read. This was too much. There was no way that anyone in their right mind could possibly think that she'd believe it was real.

It was crazy. The fact that someone would even think of a lie this absurd...

Her gaze fell on the pages. They looked so real, but they couldn't be. They had to be fake. Those reports couldn't be true.

Could they?

4

The nightmares were back in full force. She woke up suddenly to Vaughn shaking her, her heart racing and her breath coming in frantic gasps. Vaughn was staring at her, his white eyes full of concern.

She looked around the room, trying to get her bearings as her breathing slowed down.

"That was a bad one," Vaughn said quietly. "Are you okay?"

She swallowed hard before nodding. "Thank you for waking me up."

"Do you want to talk about it?"

She felt her body tense up. When she was with Tecken she had to report on her dreams so that Wes could monitor the reassignment and make sure she wasn't starting to remember. But she wasn't with Tecken, and it was perfectly okay for Vaughn to ask. Anyone who was trying to make their partner feel better would ask such a thing. It wasn't a sign of something sinister.

She shook her head. "I just want to forget it."

He nodded and didn't push her.

She took in a few deep breaths, trying to think of anything other than the dream, but it was difficult to forget something so horrifying. Someone else had taken control of her body, and she was trapped in her mind, unable to stop herself from doing anything, and only able to watch in horror. She could see herself being obedient to Erikson, following his plans and offering to help in any way. Then the dream moved to the war, showing her injuring people and causing massive destruction with her powers, demolishing building and ripping open streets. But that wasn't the worst part. As the destruction escalated, she could only watch as her body attacked her friends. Confusion crossed their faces as she betrayed them, using her powers against them. Zenyth, Naydir, Bryanna, and Cale all lay before her, bleeding and unmoving. The sound of wicked laughter escaped her mouth as she turned on Vaughn, who was standing in stunned silence at the horror before him. His expression remained unchanged as she aimed a killing blow.

She knew that it was just a dream, but it felt so real, so plausible. She didn't want to tell anyone about this terrible thing that her mind had created – she wanted it out of her mind as fast as possible.

Vaughn's hand was on her back, moving in slow, comforting circles. Usually that was enough to calm her down, but this nightmare had shaken her to her core. She should tell him about it, just like she should have told him about the letters, but every time she opened her mouth, something held her back.

She put on an appreciative smile and turned to him. "Thank you for waking me up."

"Do you want to try going back to sleep?" he asked gently.

She nodded, afraid that if she spoke her voice would betray her fear.

They lay down and she moved so close to him that she

could hear his breathing and feel his chest rise and fall. Keeping
her face hidden, she tried to relax her body, but every now and
then an image would flash in her mind and she'd feel a tightness
in her chest.

Eventually Vaughn's breath settled into a rhythm and she
knew that he'd fallen asleep. She envied him. He'd never done
anything so terrible in his life. Even though he'd said he wanted
to be there for her, he could never understand what it was like
to be in her mind. He couldn't help her. Nobody could.

CHAPTER 19

"Big meeting in five minutes," Lei remarked as she walked past Zenyth's desk.

Zenyth looked up from her paperwork and nodded appreciatively. Her brain had been so focused on the task at hand that she hadn't realized almost an hour had gone by.

It would have been terrible if she'd been late for the meeting. Nobody in the office knew what it was about but they all had their theories: the most popular of which involved the current rumours swirling around regarding the possible registration of Elementals. The opinion column had been printing letters on both sides for the past week, but the ISS had yet to make any kind of official statement. Some people took the silence as proof that the idea was stupid, while others argued it was proof that they were considering the option.

Zenyth wished that the ISS would get off their butts and do something. She'd already had to deal with shouting matches in the street, and it was only a matter of time before tempers escalated further. Sources said that there was going to be a protest in front of the ISS building tomorrow, so maybe that would spur them into action.

Putting her paperwork aside, she headed into the briefing room, along with the other officers. Naydir was already inside, sitting on the other side of the room, and they exchanged a brief nod before Zenyth sat down. Everyone made idle chat, speculating, while they waited for the Chief. When he finally walked in, they all sat up straighter and readied their attention.

"I know that you're all curious about assignments for the protest tomorrow, and those will be posted later today," Chief Azeil began, "but that's not why I've gathered you here today. There's going to be a new initiative coming in from the ISS. It turns out that the newspaper assignment was a test, to see if we'd pick up on anything, and some of us happened to pass."

Zenyth sat up even straighter.

"The ISS already noticed that the number of Elemental crimes in Briton was strangely high and wanted to find out if others thought the same way. Two of our officers happened to bring it to my attention, so I'd like to thank Officer Keen for mentioning it to me, and Officer Z. Hansen for writing up a ten-page report."

He glanced over at Zenyth, who gave him a nod.

"Now that it's been confirmed that there is a problem, we'll need to keep a closer eye on the Briton crime pages, comparing reports and tracking issues on the island. Reading all of the Segment papers will continue, so thank you for your patience on this matter. In the meanwhile, the ISS will be coming up with a plan to send officers to Briton in order to investigate these matters further. I'd like you all to think about whether or not you'd like to help with this task – especially you two, Keen and Hansen. We don't know exactly what it will entail at the moment, and it might last weeks or years, but it will go a long way towards creating a fair environment on Briton. Thank you for your time. You may all go back to work."

The Chief left and the staff started to file out of the room.

"Congratulations, Z," Naydir said as he made his way over

to her. "You're going to make the rest of us look bad."

"Hey, you had as much opportunity as I did," she informed him.

He gave her shoulder a quick squeeze of support before walking away.

As Zenyth walked over to her desk, Lei fell into step beside her.

"So, you thinking of signing up for the transfer?" Lei asked.

"Maybe," Zenyth shrugged. "I guess it depends on what kind of operation they're hoping to run."

"I think you should do it anyway. Ten-page report..." Lei laughed to herself. "Heck, I barely gave it any thought, even after you brought it up."

"That's only because you don't think that people are inherently terrible."

Lei laughed again and headed to her desk.

≈

Later that day, as she was walking home from her judo class, Zenyth wondered if she should offer to go to Briton. It had been fun to imagine being a spy again, but now that it might become a reality, she had to put serious thought into it. The Chief had mentioned her by name, so there was no hiding behind indecision. Besides, what was keeping her on Stanton? Naydir had a life of his own and her friends were doing fine, and it wasn't like she was staying here for anyone. As much as she liked her judo and boxing classes, they weren't a reason to put off making a change. She'd always imagined her future being with her brother, but now that he had gone on his own path what was stopping her from doing something different?

It wasn't that long ago that she'd been hoping for some kind of project to sink her teeth into, and now there was one right in front of her. Sure, the Chief had once said that she was as subtle as a brick wall, but he wouldn't have suggested she sign up if he didn't think she could handle it. Besides, nobody knew yet what the ISS was planning for this operation. They might want covert spies or they might want more obvious plants, so there could be a spot that would be perfect for her.

It would be tough to travel to a new island where she didn't know anyone, especially when that island was Briton, but after everything she'd been through, she could handle tough.

CHAPTER 20

The envelope was staring at her.

Everywhere Kit moved in the living room, she could see the envelope, sitting innocently on the coffee table with the rest of the mail. Even when she went into to the kitchen, she could feel its presence, calling out to her, begging her to come back and open it up.

It didn't help that she hadn't slept last night. After that terrible nightmare, she couldn't bring herself to close her eyes. At work she'd tried her hardest to act like a functioning human being, but there were times when she was alone in her office when it was impossible to keep the act up anymore, and she could only stare at the wall, waiting for her workday to end.

When it was time to go home, she felt miserable. A few co-workers had asked if she was coming down with something, confirming her suspicions that she looked as bad as she felt. All she wanted to do was sleep, but images from the nightmare continued to haunt her. If only there was some way to guarantee that she wouldn't dream.

Vaughn must have gotten the mail before going out for the afternoon, because he wasn't in the apartment when she arrived home from work. When she saw the envelope sitting on the coffee table, she instantly froze. After finally gaining control of herself, she went into the kitchen to make a cup to tea, but the thought of what that envelope might contain wouldn't leave her alone. Knowing that its existence would haunt her no matter where she went, she returned to the living room, where she sat cross-legged on the couch, holding her cup of tea and staring at it.

When Vaughn arrived home, she hadn't moved. She didn't know how much time had passed, but her half-finished tea had gone cold. When Vaughn saw her sitting there, the concerned look reappeared on his face. That look was showing up a lot these days.

"Rough day?" he asked gently.

Judging from his tone, she must have looked even worse than she thought.

"Did you see the paper today?" she said, thinking back to the opinion piece she'd read earlier.

He nodded. "It wasn't the nicest thing the paper's ever printed."

"Maybe they're right," she remarked, looking out the window. "Maybe I *am* an abomination of nature. I mean, Tecken did a ton of tests and couldn't figure out how I exist. Even science wants nothing to do with me."

Vaughn sat down next to her. "Maybe science just needs to catch up. They'll start learning more, and one day they'll figure it out."

She scoffed. "I'll probably be long dead by then."

"Kit, you're not an abomination." He put an arm around her. "Trust me, because I'd know if you were."

"But I've done such terrible..." She felt tears starting to well up in her eyes. She'd only mentioned that stupid article because she didn't want to talk to him about the letters – she didn't think it would bring back all her regrets.

He didn't say anything, just continued to hold her. It should have been enough.

She let out a sigh. "It's difficult sometimes... To separate what I am from what people think I am. Maybe it would have been better if I'd left after the war and gone someplace where nobody knows me... Maybe I was an idiot to think I could live a normal life."

"These articles are stupid, and they'll stop eventually. People will find something else to focus on."

"If only that could be guaranteed," she muttered.

"Why don't we talk about what we should make for supper and get your mind off of things that you shouldn't waste time focusing on?

He stood up and held out his hand. Giving him a weak smile, she took it and he helped her to her feet. While they walked to the kitchen, he talked about all the different things they could make, making each of the options sound better and more exciting than the last. She found herself smiling, and it strengthened her resolve to forget about all the terrible things that had been haunting her and focus on the happiness she had.

And for a while it worked. Chopping vegetables and talking about books and movies, it felt as if her life had returned to normal.

"Any plans for tonight?" she asked him as they washed the dishes.

"I was thinking of a little photography followed by some late-night developing in my studio, but it can wait."

"I don't want you to give up on your plans, but how about you cut the developing short, and we watch a really stupid movie later tonight? I can make popcorn."

He smiled. "Sounds like a plan. What are you going to do until then?"

She shrugged. "Maybe read something. Try to distract myself from the rest of the world."

He gave her a kiss on top of her head. "Well, I wish you the best of luck with that."

Vaughn left shortly after, grabbing his camera bag on the way out. Once he was gone, Kit sat in the living room and picked up the book she was currently reading. Although it was an interesting story about someone travelling through every island in Segment Alpha, she was finding it hard to focus. Maybe it had something to do with the envelope that was still staring at her.

When she realized that she'd read the same page three times over and still had no idea what was going on, she decided that it was futile to keep trying. She needed something better to distract her – she needed a hobby. A few years ago she'd tried knitting, but gave up after continual mistakes in reading the patterns and constantly dropping stitches. She didn't know what to do with the things she'd made, since there weren't many people who'd want a scarf of inconsistent widths that was full of holes. Maybe if she'd stuck with it, she'd have gotten better, but that could have taken years.

Finally, after glaring at the envelope, she decided to go for a walk. Usually she tried to stay inside and avoid contact with other people, but every once in a while the restlessness became too much and she had to get out. At first, she'd tried suppressing the urge, but it made her overly irritable. Eventually she'd give in and go outside, which would be great – for a while. She'd soon get tired of the staring and whispering, and her resolve to stay inside would return.

Going for a walk sounded like a dumb idea, considering all those opinion pieces about her that were floating around in the paper, but right now she'd rather deal with people staring and whispering instead of sitting here with that stupid envelope begging to be opened. Pulling a hat over her blue hair, Kit took a few deep breaths and left the apartment.

She wandered aimlessly for a while, walking along the streets closer to the water, taking in the fresh air. At first she was overly paranoid about people recognizing her, but the people she encountered didn't seem to pay her much attention and some of the tension that she normally felt when she was out in public began to disappear.

She wandered downtown, going into a bookstore to see if there was anything interesting to read, but nothing grabbed her attention. She passed by stores, looking in through the windows to see if they were selling anything that she might be able to pick up as a hobby. After considering a few ideas, like painting or writing or woodworking, Kit realized that she wasn't particularly interested in finding a new hobby. What she really enjoyed doing was going for walks, so she gave up on shopping and continued to wander.

As she walked, she wondered what her life would have been like if she'd stayed on Aesira after graduating. Would her powers still be a secret? Would the Second Invasion have happened? Would she be happier?

The reports from Tecken hovered in the back of her mind. Was it possible that Aesira was a lie? She could remember being in school, but was that a false memory or a real one? Time had caused her memories to fade, but that happened to everyone. It was a normal thing and didn't mean that the memories were less valid. Aesira was true. This was her real life.

Despite her assertiveness, the merest thought of the Tecken reports chased away her happy mood. She wondered if the people around her could sense the turmoil that was going on inside of her head. Nobody seemed to be staring at her, but it wouldn't be difficult for them to turn away whenever she looked in their direction. Her skin started to crawl with paranoia, and she decided to head back to the apartment.

Vaughn wasn't home yet, so she figured that she might as well clean up, hoping that the physical exercise would distract her. She didn't want to deal with the living room and the envelope, so she started in the kitchen, washing the dirty dishes and wiping down the counters. From there she moved on to the bathroom, and then the bedroom, tidying up small messes and putting things in order. When she finally looked at the clock, she realized that it was past the time Vaughn said he'd be home. He must have lost track of time in his studio again. Some nights she never knew if she should bother waiting up for him or if she should give up and go to bed.

A knock on the door interrupted her cleaning, but the distraction was a welcome one. She wondered who would be knocking at this time of night. Maybe Vaughn had forgotten his keys.

When she opened the door, Sav was on the other side. His face was heavy with worry, and she wondered what had happened.

"Sav, what's wrong?" she asked.

He swallowed hard. "I just got a call from Naydir. It's Vaughn. There's been an accident."

CHAPTER 21

The scene was all too familiar. The stark white walls of the hospital room; Vaughn lying on the bed, covered by a white blanket, unmoving except for the rise and fall of his chest.

Sixteen years ago, Vaughn ended up in the hospital after Nathan wounded him with an illegal gun, making Vaughn the first gunshot victim in Stanton in almost a century. No one knew what kind of damage the bullet would do, and Kit had been terrified that he wouldn't make it. It had felt like her fault, since she had willingly gone with Nathan in an effort to try and find out where the Tecken base was and Vaughn was only there because he'd followed them. Even though Vaughn had said that it was his fault for not letting her handle things on her own, he never would have gotten shot if she hadn't been stupid enough to think she could handle something that was so obviously a trap.

Looking at Vaughn now, with bandages wrapped around his left arm and his head, Kit couldn't help recalling another terrible memory of how she had burned him while she was under Tecken's control and almost killed him during the war. It made her question yet again why he was still with her. How had he been able to forgive her for everything she'd done?

She'd been too in shock to drive, so Sav drove them to the

hospital. Naydir had been waiting for them, and when they arrived, he took her in to see Vaughn, filling her in on what had happened.

"There was an explosion at his studio, probably something happened with his chemicals. He was found unconscious in the front room by a citizen who noticed the smoke, and they managed to get him to safety before the fire did any real damage."

As soon as Kit walked into Vaughn's room, Naydir's words had become distant, falling into the background. How could there have been an accident? Vaughn was always so careful with his supplies. Had he been rushing to get back home? Was it her fault again that he was injured?

She walked over to Vaughn and took his hand in hers, relieved that he felt warm and alive. The doctors had already treated his head wound and the burns, and his left arm was wrapped in bandages from the wrist to the upper arm. His breathing was steady, but his eyes remained closed and there was no reaction.

"The doctors say that he could wake up in an hour or a week or later," Naydir said. "Head wounds are difficult to judge, and they don't know how much force was behind the explosion."

Tears began to fill Kit's eyes, but she knew she needed to pull herself together. She didn't know if the current situation was making her cry or if it was because of all her guilty memories. Maybe it was some strange combination of both. She tried to remind herself that this was nothing more than a terrible accident.

Time lost all meaning as she stood there, holding Vaughn's hand and willing him to wake up. Eventually Naydir came over to her and said that they should go home. She carefully placed Vaughn's hand back on the bed and allowed Naydir to lead her out of the room.

As Naydir drove Sav and her back to the apartment building, everyone remained silent. Kit wasn't sure if they were waiting for her to speak or if enough had been said on the matter.

"Would you like me to come in for a while?" Naydir asked as they reached the third floor.

She shook her head.

"Well, I'm only next door if you need me." But he didn't walk away. He stood in the hallway, Sav standing close by, keeping a careful eye on her as she entered her apartment.

When she shut the door, leaving them in the hallway, she heard Naydir's words echo in her head. He was just along the hallway, right next to her, in the perfect location to keep an eye on her. It was very convenient, wasn't it?

She quickly shook that thought out of her head. As much as she wanted to think about anything other than Vaughn's unmoving form, she knew that particular line of thought wouldn't be helpful. Instead she tried to think of all the things she could find comfort in – that Vaughn was still alive, that he had been found in time, and that he could wake up at any minute.

As she walked through the apartment, she wondered what time it was. It had to be late, but she wasn't feeling tired. If anything, she felt numb, as if her emotions had been used up, leaving her hollow inside.

ᴎ

The streets of Stanton were empty. There had to be people somewhere, but she couldn't see or hear anyone. It was deathly quiet.

There was no specific path that she walked, choosing to take whichever turn called out to her whenever she reached a fork in the road. The buildings rose around her as she walked, like dark grey monoliths, growing taller and taller until she could barely see the sky.

A noise to her left caught her attention and she moved towards it. As she turned a corner, she saw two men fighting. They were about the same height, but one had yellow hair and was holding a gun, while the other had red hair and a long sword. The red-haired man knocked the other down and held the blade to his throat. She cried out and raced forward, using her power to set the man's coat on fire before he could kill his opponent. He quickly dropped the sword and backed away. Throwing a gust of wind forward, she knocked the red-haired man back against a wall with a sickening 'thud'. He slid to the ground, unconscious, and she turned her attention to the blond haired man. As he stood up, he smiled at her, and she felt a smile cross her own lips.

"Thanks for that," he said. "Guess I got myself into some trouble. But don't worry…" He walked over to the unconscious man and aimed the gun at his head.

She watched as the unconscious man's hair mixed with the blood pooling underneath his head. He looked familiar, but she didn't know why.

There was a loud 'bang' as the man standing next to her pulled the trigger. The red-haired man went deathly still and the street was silent once more.

The yellow haired man held his hand out to her. She looked up into his red eyes, which were full of happiness. She took his hand and it was so strong and warm. It felt like home.

'*This,*' she thought, '*this is where I belong.*'

Kit woke up in a cold sweat. She had fallen asleep on the couch and for a few seconds she didn't know where she was. Once she got her bearings, the details of the dream came back to her, and she felt cold and empty and horrified. The scene stuck in her mind like a bad memory that couldn't be forgotten. It was mostly true, but the ending was wrong – she had stopped Nathan from shooting Vaughn. Yes, it had been after she'd injured him, but when it counted, she'd protected Vaughn, she had been there for him.

The memory of the shot and the stillness from the dream flashed before her eyes and her stomach twisted. She reminded herself that it was fake.

It wasn't real.

It wasn't real.

She couldn't get back to sleep after that, which only added to the exhaustion she'd felt the day before. These nightmares were going to be the death of her. If she couldn't find some way to stop dreaming, she'd never get a good night's sleep again.

Although she'd spent a lot of time alone in the apartment, it had never been like this. In the past she knew that Vaughn would arrive home eventually, but knowing that he was lying in a hospital, unsure of when he'd wake up... It made the apartment seem emptier and lonelier than ever before. She couldn't help fearing that he might never walk through the door again.

She'd been to his studio, in the South-East part of the island, many times before. Vaughn had lived there when he first moved to Stanton, leaving behind the army and his family for a new, uncertain life. She liked to refer to it as his second home, but truthfully it was his first home. She couldn't believe that something so terrible had happened there. Bad things shouldn't happen in a place where you felt safe.

Later that morning, Naydir came over to see if she wanted to go back to the hospital.

"There's nothing I can do," she said, shaking her head. She was worried that if she went back there, she would break down completely. Every time she closed her eyes, she could see the image of Nathan pulling the trigger and Vaughn's body going deathly still.

Naydir must have noticed how difficult this was for her, because he didn't ask any questions or try to guilt her into going to the hospital. Instead he gave her an update on Vaughn's injuries. There had been some shrapnel from the blast, but it was nothing serious, and the doctors were confident there would be no infection. The burns on his arm were from his sleeve catching fire, but they were only second-degree burns, not third. Being on the ground meant that he probably hadn't inhaled much of the smoke or chemicals, so their only real concern was the head wound.

After Naydir filled her in, he seemed to realize that she wasn't in the mood for company. Before leaving he said that he would call her workplace to let them know what had happened and tell them that she wouldn't be in for a few days. Then, giving one last sympathetic look, he left.

As soon as he was gone, the apartment went back to being empty and cavernous. She didn't want to do anything, but she also didn't want to sit here and stare into space. Maybe she should clean again or try baking something or rearrange her books.

Her gaze fell on the envelope, which was still sitting untouched on the table. Her mind was already in a vulnerable state, so opening this would definitely be a bad idea. It would only confuse an already confusing situation, and she needed to think about what she could be doing for Vaughn, even if the answer was nothing.

These were all the thoughts she told herself in an effort to leave the envelope alone. She knew that her mind was right, and she should stop staring at it and leave the room. She should do something – anything that didn't involve looking at this thing which was certain to contain terrible lies.

But… But what if they weren't lies.

What if the letters were true? What if the reports were real and she'd actually grown up on Tecken? Was it possible to erase someone's mind so completely that they couldn't remember anything? Was that why she couldn't forget her memories of Tecken, because they were what truly belonged in her mind?

What if the envelope in front of her held the key?

She couldn't stop her hand from moving forward. The envelope was like the previous, definitely containing more than one page. Holding onto it, it suddenly felt like there was a large pit inside of her stomach. What stories would these pages tell?

It felt as if someone else was controlling her movements, as she opened the envelope and removed its contents. There were three pages in all, dry and aged, but not as yellow as the others.

Each page had a stamp of the ISS logo in the top left corner.

Her breath caught in her throat. She'd been expecting more Tecken pages – pages that could have been forged by Tecken soldiers ages ago. She was definitely not expecting this.

Mission Report 8934. RE: Project Six. Our reassignment strategy has failed again. In the interest of time, it has been decided that we shall have to resort to our secondary strategy. Preparations have already been completed, and all of the necessary parts have been put together and fabricated. Although it will be an arduous task, if it works, we shall have full control. We are aware of the possible consequences, but we must sever the connection to Tecken no matter what the cost. It is obvious that having such power on our side would be an enormous benefit, but if the secondary reassignment fails, at least we will have kept this power out of Tecken's hands. Authorization has already been given, and we will commence with this strategy in T-12 hours.

End Report.

Mission Report 9104. RE: Project Six. The Reassignment is still holding. We have gone one week without any visible issues. Although it has been suggested that we bring the subject in for another session, it has been decided that we will hold off for now and only intervene if it becomes necessary. It is only a matter of time before we move to phase two. All of the pieces are in place and ready. Each employee has been given their duty and script and have been instructed on what to watch for. Once phase two has been put into motion, we shall see about moving to phase three.

End Report.

Mission Report 9217. RE: Project Six. We have heard reports that Tecken has placed soldiers on the island. Although this does not change phase two, it slightly complicates matters. We suspect that they are searching for the subject, but are confident that our reassignment will not be broken. Reports from our employees say that the reassignment is holding fast and that the subject does not suspect anything in the slightest. We may have to postpone phase three for now, until we can confirm the presence of Tecken spies.

End Report.

The reports didn't say anything specific, but Kit could read between the lines. They were talking about brainwashing someone – someone powerful, who had once been on Tecken's side, and who the ISS would rather have on their side. Someone who might have some significance to the number six. It made sense that the ISS would keep any specifics out of the reports, in case they were discovered by someone who wasn't a part of the project, but even then it wasn't hard to work out what they might be talking about.

Maybe she was reading too much into this, but she doubted it. It matched up too perfectly with the previous reports from Tecken. Was it possible that these papers were real? If they were, then it confirmed the idea that she had originally been on Tecken's side and had been manipulated to join the ISS. As strange as that idea was, the more evidence she received, the more plausible it sounded.

She had been the one to kill Magnus Erikson after all – and end his family line. Had she done it because there was no other way to end the war or because she was a puppet of the ISS? She could have incapacitated him and taken him in, but instead her instinct had been to take him down and finally end Erikson's control over Tecken. A small voice inside her head had told her that he was dangerous and that he and his descendants wouldn't stop until the whole world was under their control, but when she thought about it, Erikson had only ever talked about ruling the Segment, not the world. So where had that thought come from? Had it been planted by the ISS, to make her do what they wanted? If they could plant a lifetime of false memories, something like that would be easy enough to slip in.

Despite earlier reservations, she was beginning to believe the letters. Ever since she'd signed up to help the ISS, she'd been under their thumb. They had made the team move to a house together, so that they could reach everyone easier, but strategically it seemed like a bad idea to put all your spies under one roof. Or had everyone else been put there to keep an eye on her?

Naydir and Zenyth didn't require the security that she did, so why were they living in the ISS apartment building? Why were they next door to her? How had it been so easy for Zenyth to find another apartment on the same floor?

Had Cale and Bryanna moved away because they wanted a change or because their jobs had finished?

And Vaughn... What if Vaughn was only with her because he was a spy for the ISS? It would make sense. There were days when she was certain that she didn't deserve him and that he'd leave her, but he never did. He was always so kind and caring, even when she was making his life miserable. Maybe it was because he'd been ordered to be that way.

She hated how plausible everything sounded. If it wasn't true, then why was her whole life so convenient? Why had she not talked to her mother or her step-sisters in over a decade? Mich and Jill were now twenty-three and twenty-four, so they were adults who could make up their own minds: and although she couldn't risk phoning or visiting her mother, she had always thought that her step-sisters would contact her once they'd broken away from their father's tyrannical rule. Instead, there was only silence. Kit assumed that they had fallen prey to the teachings of the Humanists and that they still lived on Briton, but what if that wasn't true? What if they had never existed? What if they had been part of an elaborate lie – a reason to make her not question her lack of family?

After the Second Invasion her friends had helped her realize what was real and what wasn't, but maybe that was their purpose. They were there to reassure her that the Tecken memories were all false and that this was where she belonged. It made sense.

Suddenly Kit was overwhelmed with the feeling that she might burst into tears. Yes, her life was difficult, but it was *her* life. To find out that it was false and that everyone she'd ever cared about was lying to her and pretending to be her friend... It was more than she could take.

But what was she supposed to do now that she'd learned the truth? She couldn't let anyone know what she'd found out. They might bring her back to the ISS, and then they'd mess around with her brain more than they already had. She had to pretend that nothing was wrong, that she was still under their control.

A small voice in the back of her mind spoke up and made her pause. What if it wasn't the truth? What if she was allowing herself to be manipulated by these papers? They might be fakes. They might be really convincing fakes.

Before doing anything rash, she needed to find out what was real and what wasn't, but who could she trust? She couldn't go to Zenyth or Naydir, or anyone who might be involved with the ISS. Even if he wasn't in a coma, she wouldn't be able to trust Vaughn. No matter how sincere he seemed, how would she know that he was telling the truth?

Her chest began to feel tight, and she put her hands on the couch, feeling a sudden need to touch something real. The fabric was soft and sturdy – it was real and so was she. If only it was that easy to know which memories were real. Why didn't she have any photographs from her past? What happened to that picture of her and her dad? Had she lost it, or had it never existed in the first place?

The tightness in her chest increased as her entire world started crumbling around her.

CHAPTER 22

A pile of newspapers were sitting on her desk, but Zenyth couldn't bring herself to read them. At this very moment, Vaughn was lying in the hospital, still unconscious. The incident had happened while she was off work, so she'd heard about it from Naydir, who had been working the late shift. She'd been getting ready for bed when the phone rang, which was the first clue that something terrible had happened. Nobody ever called her that late. She'd considered going to the hospital, but quickly realized that there was nothing she'd be able to do.

When she arrived at work that morning, she hunted down as much information on the fire as possible. Most people assumed it had been an accident; that some of the chemicals stored in the studio had mixed and gone volatile, but she wasn't so sure. Vaughn had been a photographer for a long time and he was careful with his materials.

The part that scared her was how isolated Vaughn's studio was. It was in an older area of the island, near small businesses that weren't usually occupied at night. If that person hadn't been in the area at the right time, noticed the fire, and pulled Vaughn to safety... She didn't want to think about what might have been.

She couldn't think of any reason that anyone would have

for wanting to hurt Vaughn, unless it was another artist who was jealous of his work. But would someone take that jealousy so far as to try to kill him? Maybe someone had simply gone out for a bit of nighttime arson and they didn't realize that someone was inside the building or what it contained.

The police would have to investigate the matter, as they did for all accidents. Although Zenyth trusted her co-workers she was worried that if they went in there not suspecting foul play, they might miss something. She needed to get put on that team.

When she knocked on the chief's door, he didn't seem particularly surprised to see her.

"Anything on your mind, Hansen?" he asked, gesturing to the chair across from his desk.

She shook her head at the seat and remained standing. "There's something I'd like to talk to you about."

"Go on."

"It's about the explosion on the South-East end yesterday. You'll need to put together a team to investigate and I'd like to be on it."

The chief sat back in his chair. "If I recall correctly, you're friends with the man who owns that studio and who was caught in the explosion."

She nodded.

"You know that we don't usually put friends or family on cases. It muddies the water."

"I know, Sir, but I can keep an impartial mind, if that's what you're worried about. I only want to make sure that every possibility is examined."

"I see..." He paused again, thinking the matter over.

He thought for a long enough time that Zenyth wondered if he was deliberately trying to make her second-guess her request. She could think of a few times when they'd had people work cases involving their friends, so it wasn't such a strange request for her to make, and if she had to, she'd bring those cases up to prove her point.

Finally, he cleared his throat. "I suspect that if I don't put you on this team, you'll be spending all your free time gathering every single report and piece of evidence to go over."

He was right, but she didn't say anything.

"I'll put you on point. However, if I hear one word that you're following another agenda or abusing your power to search for clues that aren't there, I'll have you back on desk duty so fast that it'll make your head spin."

Zenyth nodded gratefully. "Thank you, Chief. I won't let you down."

"Now, before you leave, have you given any thought to the Briton Assignment?"

For a second, she was taken aback. Vaughn's accident had pushed every other thought out of her mind, and there was no way she could think about leaving while Vaughn was lying in the hospital. "Well, I had been thinking about it before all this happened."

"I'd really like you to consider going over. I know how hard you work, and I think the team would benefit from having you on it. But we can talk about it after this investigation is over."

"Thank you, Chief."

He waved his hand to dismiss her, and she quickly left the office.

≈

The investigation started that afternoon. A couple of eyebrows had been raised when Zenyth was announced as the lead, but nobody wanted to question the chief. Naydir gave her a supportive nod, but didn't say anything.

When she first saw the state of Vaughn's studio, she was careful to keep her emotions in check. She didn't think about what it used to look like or how Vaughn had been lying unconscious while the fire raged around him. Instead she thought about the usual protocol for suspicious fires and formed a plan in her mind.

First she sent Officer Decker around the outside of the building, to see if she could find anything suspicious. Then she took the rest of the team inside, giving them information about the studio as they walked through. The first room was a waiting area, left over from the building's previous days as a business, with three doors along the back wall. These led to a bathroom, a dark room, and a storage room. Zenyth knew that Vaughn stored most of his materials in the storage room, but they were put to use in the dark room. Although there were burns all over the room, the patterns seemed to point to the storage room as the place of ignition.

The team arrived at the same conclusion, but she told them to keep their eyes open for anything that might contradict that theory before splitting them up and assigning them each an area in which to take photographs and gather samples. She didn't take an area for herself, choosing instead to float around and make sure her team was working hard.

As she walked around the back of the building, she saw Decker taking photographs of a huge burn mark on the wall.

"What do you think about that?" Zenyth asked her.

Decker lowered her camera. "Well, it looks like a possible ignition point, since the burn's so tall and charred. Someone could have set the wall on fire out here, or it might have resulted from the ignition point being on the other side."

"I'm pretty sure the storage room is on the other side. I'll make sure we take note of any chemicals or materials that might have been stored against this wall."

Zenyth left Decker and decided to check out the storage room. If there were no combustible materials close to the wall, then that could rule out an accident. It would be helpful if they found fire-starting materials outside the studio, but even the absence of matches wouldn't prove that it hadn't been arson. Any Fire Elemental could have started the blaze with a thought, leaving no evidence behind.

Even though she thought that arson was more likely than carelessness, Zenyth still couldn't come up with a valid reason why anyone would want to hurt Vaughn like this. Why had this building been set on fire? Why last night? Was it a terrible mistake that someone had been inside or did the arsonist deliberately set the fire while Vaughn was there?

In the storage area, Officer Hale was taking meticulous photographs. Nothing had been touched yet, and nothing would be until it had all been categorized. She decided to leave Hale to his work and see how the rest of the team was doing.

The work went slow, but they were careful, taking all of the necessary photos before they started moving things around and taking samples. Zenyth made sure that every sample collected was properly tagged and carefully packed in the police car.

Most fires that they investigated were on a much smaller scale, and the bigger fires were usually in homes and didn't need much investigating. This place had chemicals and equipment, and a lot of items that needed to be tagged and sampled. Nothing about this job would be easy.

As Zenyth watched her team work, she knew that they had a long day ahead of them.

CHAPTER 23

The phone was ringing, but Kit was too focused on her task to register the sound. Spread out on the floor in front of her were all the letters she had received from Wes, along with a multitude of pages filled with handwritten memories. The pages contained everything she could remember about her life, from growing up on Briton all the way to yesterday. She'd written down every recollection of her time in university on Aesira, when she'd moved to Stanton, and then working for the ISS – everything she'd regarded as her real life. After that, she moved into her memories of being brainwashed by Tecken and everything that had happened while she'd thought she was one of them, along with the events of the Second Invasion. It had taken her days to sort through all of her thoughts and she still wasn't finished. Every now and then she'd remember an odd detail and would have to pause to write it down before it was forgotten. Her hand was aching from the non-stop writing, but she couldn't allow herself to take a break.

The act of writing had become almost trance-like. She hadn't been sleeping well, but that was par for the course. A few times last night she'd found herself startled awake, so she must have slept a bit. Thankfully there were no memories of dreams, which was a welcome relief. Maybe her brain was too overworked and

had decided to shut down while she slept, or maybe it had realized that the reality of her life was worse than anything it could
come up with. Whatever the case might be, she'd take it. Her
head was muddled enough without any strange dreams adding
to the confusion.

At first she'd tried to keep the memories in chronological
order, but as more and more pages were added to the pile, it
grew difficult to figure out the exact order of certain events. The
piles became larger and messier, and after a few days she gave
up and vowed to sort them later.

The phone finally went quiet. She continued to write, pen
moving as fast as possible over the page, not stopping to correct
spelling mistakes or missed words. There was a pause as she
tried to remember a detail that was missing, but it appeared that
particular piece of information was gone for now and the pen
was put back to paper.

It was late afternoon when she finally finished, putting the
paper and pen down and letting out a huge sigh. As she mas-
saged her tired hand, she tried to make sense of everything in
front of her.

This exercise had brought back a lot of memories, but not
one single memory of growing up on Tecken. She remembered
being in the park with her parents, and her father reading bed-
time stories to her, but that had all happened in Briton. Briton
had to be the true memory. It was where her father's memorial
was, after all.

But why don't you ever visit the memorial? a voice in the back
of her mind asked. She tried to think of the last time she'd gone
there, but it had been long before her mother had remarried.
In fact, she may have visited it only once, during the farewell
ceremony. It had been difficult to look at it, knowing that the
small plaque represented all that was left of her father. Even as

a child, she'd only wanted to remember his life, not his death.

Shaking the doubt out of her head, she tried to get back on track. There weren't many details of her past that were specific to Briton, but a lot of her memories had mostly faded to vagaries. It made sense, since it had been over a decade since she'd been on the island. She'd also deliberately tried to suppress a lot of her memories after her mother remarried a Humanist.

It was possible that the ISS had decided to overwrite all of her Tecken memories with memories of Briton. She wasn't sure how someone would achieve that kind of thing, but she also had no idea how any of the reassignment techniques worked and she'd experienced them first-hand. Maybe the ISS had put in a bunch of new memories that were terrible, to ensure that she wouldn't focus on them. It made sense.

Suddenly there was a knocking on her door. She jumped, but didn't make a sound. The knocking continued, but she stayed where she was, trying to be as silent as possible. Keeping her eyes on the door, she counted the knocks in her head, waiting for the person to give up, which they did after six. In the silence that followed, she continued to stare at the door, waiting to make sure that the person didn't come back. It was probably Naydir or Sav, checking up on her. She knew that she should answer their calls and let them know that she was all right, but they'd probably want to spend time with her, and she needed every available second to figure this mystery out. She'd talk to them once she knew whether or not she could trust them.

The knocking had been enough to distract her and she realized how long it had been since she'd eaten anything. Being careful to move quietly, she stood up and went to the kitchen to make a quick snack.

If only there was some way she could know for certain what was real and what wasn't. She had a lot of memories, but it was entirely possible that all of them were fake and that this exercise would prove nothing. Considering how much tampering had been done to her brain, she didn't feel as if she could trust anything it came up with. Even the pages and pages of memories didn't prove anything, and in some cases they only made the matter worse. She could remember being in the park on Briton with her father, but had it actually been Briton? Could it have been Tecken instead? And that was only one of the many, many memories that existed in a strange limbo, where she had some details but not enough. For all she knew, that park could have been any island in the Segment.

How was she supposed to know which version was the truth?

What she needed to do was visit Briton and see if the parks and streets were the same as the ones in her memories, but the mere thought of visiting Briton caused her lip to curl in disgust. Her last memory of the island had been so terrible that she didn't know if she'd be able to go back there.

That feeling was very convenient.

There was something else she could do other than go to Briton, but it wasn't much better. It involved going to Tecken instead. She hadn't set foot on that island since she'd finished repairing the bridges, mostly because she was public enemy number one, for both the people who had followed Erikson and her former friend – the current Leader of Tecken – Akola Allen.

But those were her only choices – go to Tecken, risk being discovered as the Six-Elemental and run off the island, or go to Briton, risk being discovered as the Six-Elemental, and... She actually wasn't sure what would happen to her if she was discovered on Briton. As far as she knew, the Humanists were laying low, but she wouldn't put it past one of them to come out from hiding to attack her. It would probably be a big boost for them if they got rid of her. They could always say that it was an unfortunate accident or blame it on another Elemental. She'd seen a lot of crimes there get swept under the rug.

A wave of calm washed over her. What was she doing? Of course her past was the truth. All of these papers and reports were simply Wes messing with her mind. This idea that she'd been born on Tecken was absolutely ridiculous.

Laughing to herself, she started to gather up the papers from the floor. As she did, her gaze fell on the ISS reports. Her smooth calm gained a wrinkle. Wes could have done just as much damage with fake Tecken reports, but faking ISS reports would be so much more effort. And these reports didn't look fake.

Groaning, she put her head in her hands. She'd been so close to moving on, and now she was doubting everything again. She had to do it – she had to go to Tecken and see if anything there was familiar. If nothing was, then she could return to Stanton, burn all these stupid letters, and let things go back to normal. If everything was familiar, then... Well, she'd probably have a nervous breakdown in the middle of the island and lose her mind.

Either way, at least she'd finally have an answer.

ᚺ

That night she dreamed of Nathan. They were lying on the grass in a park, side by side. The sky was bright blue with only a few fat, white clouds, and the temperature was perfect.

They were talking about what they'd do after Erikson had conquered the Segment, laughing about whether they'd stay in the army or get regular jobs that didn't involve fighting with weapons. She had joked that maybe she'd become an architect and build monuments to Erikson – buildings much taller than the ISS buildings. These monuments would be so tall that the ISS would forever live in Erikson's shadow.

Nathan took her hand and looked into her eyes. "Whatever you do, I want to be there with you."

The sun shone and the scent of grass filled the air, and they kissed.

And then she woke up.

As her eyes adjusted to the darkness, she was confused why her room was so big. And why was the bed was so large? It was big enough for two people. This wasn't her room in the base. Where was she?

Suddenly she realized that she was on Stanton. The side of the bed that Vaughn slept on was cold and empty, and she felt a twinge of guilt for having another dream about Nathan while Vaughn was lying in the hospital.

She felt haunted by the idea that that wasn't just a strange dream, but a repressed memory. If her relationship with Nathan had only been for a few months, then why was she still dreaming about him? Why wouldn't the memories of him fade into time and leave her alone? A few months shouldn't be enough time for someone to create such a bond. Was it possible that there were other feelings that had been suppressed, that could only come out when she was sleeping?

Were her dreams trying to tell her the truth?

CHAPTER 24

There was one thing Kit needed to do before going to Tecken, but it had to be quick, before Naydir or Zenyth found her, figured out her plan, and stopped her.

As she stood in the hospital room, holding Vaughn's hand, she was torn between wanting him to wake up and wanting him to stay asleep. If he woke up right now, she didn't know if she'd be able to go through with this plan. She'd probably stay here with him, but the uncertainty would always be there, in the back of her mind, making her wonder *What if?* Maybe it was best that he stayed asleep until she'd found some answers.

If it turned out that her life on Tecken was the truth and Naydir and Zenyth had been employed by the ISS to keep an eye on her, then Kit would be heart-broken. The fact that they had pretended to be her friends for so long, all while they were simply following orders... It would be a betrayal of the trust she'd had in them.

However, if it turned out that Vaughn had been working for the ISS the entire time, she would be destroyed.

She wanted Tecken to be a lie. She wanted to go to the island and feel completely out of place and return home to her normal life full of surety. Then she could forget about those papers and the letters, and live the rest of her life in peace.

But in order to do that, she first had to find out the truth.

Placing Vaughn's hand back on the bed, she kissed him on the cheek, gave him one last look, and left the room.

ท

It had been over a decade since Kit had set foot on Tecken. Although she'd felt like the wronged party, having been kidnapped and brainwashed, it didn't stop the people of that island from hating her. She thought she understood why they felt that way, but now she wondered it they were angry because she'd killed Erikson or disappointed that she'd forgotten about her past and betrayed them.

Driving along the highway in her El-car, she kept an eye out for anyone that might be following her. It was possible that the ISS had eyes on her, watching her every move. Her thoughts were the height of paranoia, but she wasn't in the healthiest mindset at the moment. Her suspicions were already too far gone.

She'd placed a hat over her hair and made sure to cover up her elemental Tattoos, except for the wavy blue lines of Air on her wrist. She'd considered covering those up as well, but wearing bracelets or long-sleeves would have been more suspicious than leaving them exposed. After parking downtown, she pulled the brim of her hat low over her eyes and started to walk. Not many people she passed gave her a second glance – they were all too busy with their own lives to be concerned with her.

At first she wandered aimlessly, moving through the more crowded areas, searching for anything that might be familiar. The streets were laid in the same grid-pattern that all the other islands had, so there was no worry of getting lost. It was familiar, but she didn't know if it was because she'd been here before or if it was because all islands were laid out like this.

She walked through parks and neighbourhoods, but despite her hopes, all she saw were places that were generic enough to be the background of any of her memories. The park on 14th Street could be the one where she'd played with her friend Kira, until Kira's parents had to move to another island. Or maybe that had been the park on 36th Street. Was the small library on 38th Street the same place where she'd spent so much of her time, reading book after book? If she decided to go into the library, would she see a small reading nook in the back corner? Would the layout have changed in the past decade or would it be all wrong because it wasn't the correct place?

She continued to walk, but her mood started to darken. This wasn't giving her the concrete answers that she wanted. She'd thought that she would feel at home or completely alienated, but instead it felt like she was in some strange middle-ground. How many houses had been remodelled in the past decade? How many stores repainted or moved? How much of her past might have changed for completely normal reasons? It would have made sense to give up, head back to her car and drive back to Stanton, but for some reason she continued to walk. Lost in her thoughts, she didn't pay any attention to what streets she walked down or what buildings she passed. Instead she tried to think of some way to solve the turmoil that was going on in her mind.

When she finally pulled herself out of her own thoughts, she noticed that she was in a residential area with modest houses. After finding a signpost, she saw that she was on 7th Street, which, if she remembered correctly, was the street she'd grown up on in Briton – the street she had lived on until her mother remarried and moved them in with her step-father. Kit started to pay more attention to the houses on this street, taking in the designs and colours. It wouldn't be a big loss to find out that her mother had never married a Humanist, and that she hadn't actually spent part of her life fighting to have her voice heard. It would be better to know that her mother was happy, maybe married to someone else who was nice to her. Maybe she had step-sisters that could be the kind of people they wanted to be and didn't live under an intolerant father.

Maybe, if she didn't find any answers on this trip, then she could give up on both of her possible pasts and write one of her own. She could take a hint from the previous Six-Elemental, who'd disappeared after helping the survivors of the Last World War, choosing to live his own life free from unwanted attention.

One of the houses caught her attention, bringing her to a stop. It was a split-level and looked similar to the house she'd grown up in, with yellow paint and a bright blue door. As she looked up at the two windows above the door, she could imagine the window on the left belonging to her childhood bedroom.

It wasn't a guarantee that this was the same house, after all there were only so many designs for houses and anyone could paint one in similar colours, but it had been so long since she'd seen her childhood home. A part of her wanted this to be real. Even if someone else lived there now, being able to look at it and remember how happy she'd been with her family before her father had died... It would be good enough.

She didn't know whether to laugh or burst into tears. Taking in a deep breath, she was about to turn away when the door of the house opened. A woman with yellow hair stepped out, but she came to a sudden stop when she noticed Kit.

Startled, Kit quickly looked away and started to walk down the sidewalk, but the woman called out to her. When Kit turned around, the woman was moving towards her, studying her face.

As she neared, her eyes opened wide.

"Oh my gosh... Katherine? Is that you?"

Kit looked at the woman's face, taking in the yellow hair and the wrinkles and the green eyes. She looked very much like a woman Kit had known, but many years ago. Someone younger and happier, and sadder. Kit's mouth fell open as she struggled to find the right words.

"...Mom?"

CHAPTER 25

The report on their initial findings was taking forever to finish, but Zenyth was still determined to be thorough. This was easily going to be the longest report she'd ever written, and that was before any of the lab results came back.

The team's findings hadn't resulted in any concrete answers. The burn mark on the back of the studio was definitely where the fire had started, but they still didn't know how it had began. They were waiting on information about all of the chemicals found at the site, although Zenyth doubted that any of them would have caused such an explosion without a bit of help. It made more sense that someone had started the fire outside and that the heat had caused the chemicals to explode. Hopefully the evidence would prove her theory.

There had been no clues discovered outside the studio, which could mean that the arsonist was a Fire elemental, or that the person removed any evidence when they left, or that the evidence had burned up on its own. Either way, it would be difficult to find out who had caused the fire. Zenyth tried to think of the last time they'd had an arson case, but it had been a while. Maybe she should look up some old files, for comparison's sake.

Vaughn's injuries were another cause of confusion. The

bruising on the back of his head could have been from him being thrown back by the explosion or it could have been from someone else knocking him unconscious. If only Vaughn was awake so that she could ask him these questions.

"Found anything interesting?"

She looked up to see her brother standing next to her desk. "We found tons of stuff, but nothing jumped out at us screaming, 'I was the reason for the fire'. Still waiting on lots of lab results."

He nodded. "Lunch?"

"Of course."

She tidied up the files on her desk before leaving. Unlike her apartment, her desk was always clean and tidy. At work she wanted to impress her colleagues, while at home she wanted to be comfortable.

They headed to their favourite sandwich shop, a small place a few blocks from the station. The owner grew his own spices and had a new and interesting flavour every week. Zenyth and Naydir had their old favourites, but they always made sure to try the flavour of the week. Aside from the fun of unpredictability, the food was always amazing.

"How are you holding up?" Naydir asked, once they had purchased their meals and found a table to sit at. "Working on Vaughn's case must be hard."

"Well, it was pretty hard to go through the studio, knowing what happened to him, but I'd rather do it myself than suspect that someone else was making a mess of it." She took a bite of her sandwich, tasting sweetness and heat at the same time. It was absolutely delicious, as usual.

"I know I'm not on your team, but if you need any help, let me know."

She sighed. "Is that why you asked me here? To offer your

help? Because I can handle this."

Naydir had been going in for a bite, but he paused and looked up at his sister, annoyed. "You really think that I would ever suggest that you couldn't handle this? I know better than anyone how your brain works, and I think that investigating this matter is the most productive thing you could be doing. However, I don't want you working yourself to death."

Zenyth gave him a flat look.

"Anyway, that's not why I wanted to talk to you," he said.

"Oh, it wasn't because you wanted to 'parent' me?"

"You do realize that friends and family are allowed to show concern for one another, right?" He raised an eyebrow and she finally relented.

"Fine," she sighed. "You're being a good brother and I'm being a jerk sister. Happy?"

He nodded and took a bite of his sandwich. "Wow, this is delicious."

"I know. Anyway, you wanted to talk to me about something?"

"Oh, yeah. I'm worried about Kit. I haven't talked to her in a few days, and I don't think she's been to the hospital since the first night."

"Huh, I figure she'd spend most of her time there."

"Me too, but when I called the hospital yesterday, they said that there hadn't been many visitors. I've called her apartment and knocked on her door, but there's no answer. That would normally be enough to worry me, but before Vaughn's accident he..." Naydir paused. "He asked me to keep an eye on her."

"He what?" Zenyth put her sandwich down. "What exactly did he say?"

"He said that she was having really bad nightmares, and that she was starting to withdraw again. I thought it might be like that time a couple years ago, when she got really paranoid and refused to go outside for a week, but the way he talked about her made it sound like this might be worse."

"You don't think..."

He shook his head. "No, but I'm really worried. I mean, with all that stuff in the newspapers about registering Elementals and how terrible the Six-Elemental is, and now Vaughn's accident... What if she ran away?"

Zenyth absentmindedly picked up a stray piece of lettuce and ate it. "No. I'm sure she's still on Stanton. She doesn't have anywhere else to go."

"Well, I'm working late tonight, so if you could check on her after you finish work, I'd feel a lot better."

"Can do. And if she refuses to answer, I'll break in."

Naydir's green eyes widened. "No. Don't do that."

"But I'm a cop," she said seriously. "And if I have reason to enter a room because I suspect foul play or that someone might be injured, I can do so. It's the law." She smiled at him, but she was only partly joking.

He sighed. "Just promise me you'll knock first."

"I can't promise anything."

CHAPTER 26

The drive back to Stanton felt surreal. Kit had wanted to go to Tecken to find answers, but now that she had them, she wasn't sure how to proceed. What was a person supposed to do once they realized that their entire life was a lie?

"What are you doing here?" the yellow haired woman asked. "I thought you were living in Stanton."

"I..." Kit's mouth suddenly felt dry. "I was just walking around, and this house looked familiar and..."

Disappointment crossed the woman's face. "Oh, so you haven't..."

"I mean, you're familiar. In a way. But not everything..."

"I was just heading out to do some shopping, but if you'd like to come in and talk, I can put that off." She gestured back to the house.

Kit was hesitant, but she found herself agreeing to go with the woman. This was the moment she'd been hoping to find, and now it was here, so she had to go with it. She followed the woman she suspected of being her mother through the blue door and into the house. Kit looked around the living room, which was sparsely decorated, but comfortable and warm. She wished that it looked familiar.

"So," the woman said, sitting down in an armchair. "How much do you remember?"

"Honestly, not a lot. I've got images and vague memories, but I didn't realize that they were from… here. This house is the most concrete fact I have."

She nodded. "After they told me what had been done to you by the ISS, they mentioned that you might never remember your real life. I'd hoped that they would be able to break the ISS's conditioning, but it was too strong." She gave a small, wistful smile. "When you were back with us, for those months, I'd hoped that one day you would wake up and all of your old memories would have returned, but when you went back to the ISS, well, that dream was put away."

Kit felt sadness well up inside of her. She couldn't imagine what it would be like to know that someone you loved was still alive but had been lost to you forever.

"There were letters sent to me," Kit said. "I think they were meant to jog my memory. I don't know why they were sent now and not years ago, but the letters said a lot of things that felt true to me. I mean, I'm still really confused about a lot of things, but you're… And this house…"

Her mother nodded. "It's a bit big for one person, but I couldn't bring myself to sell it, not after your father… And then when you… It was all I had left."

Kit wanted to say something comforting or reassuring, but she was at a loss for words. She'd been hoping for one big, specific moment that would break open the dam and send everything rushing forward, but her mind was still holding back. Maybe she had hoped for too much. Maybe this was the best she could ever hope to get.

Her mother seemed to notice the disappointment. A large smile appeared on her face, despite her sad eyes. "Well, if all I get is this one visit, it's more than I thought I'd ever have."

Tears started to well up in Kit's eyes. She wanted to remember everything, to comfort her mother, but she couldn't.

"Could I..." Kit paused to collect her emotions. "Could I come back and visit?"

"Of course," her eyes softened. "It's as much your house as mine."

The tears were in danger of falling, so Kit nodded. She took a few deep breaths. "Thank you so much. You... You're exactly what I've been looking for."

4

Kit had been thinking about that conversation the entire ride home. As she neared her apartment she wondered if she should've stayed on Tecken instead of going back. Now that she knew the truth, she couldn't stand to live on Stanton any longer. As soon she was back at the apartment, she'd pack a bag and leave forever. She needed to be where she belonged.

It was early evening when Kit arrived at the apartment. She should have been hungry, but her stomach was in knots, so she decided it would be better to start packing. However, before she could get out a suitcase, there was a knock on her door. She stood in the living room, wondering if she could pretend that she wasn't home, but then a voice called out.

"Kit, I know you're in there! I saw you walk in!"

Kit sighed. Of course it would be Zenyth. Taking a deep breath, she prepared herself mentally. She couldn't let Zenyth know that she knew the truth. When she opened the door, Zenyth was standing on the other side, impatiently holding today's paper.

"Did you go to Tecken today?" were the first words out of her mouth.

"What?"

"I hope that your answer is no, because someone seeing the Six-Elemental on Tecken after this news article came out would be really bad for your image."

She shoved the paper at Kit, who somehow managed not to drop it. She hadn't bothered reading the paper for the past few days, so she had no idea what Zenyth was talking about.

Zenyth walked past her, going into the living room and sitting down. Kit shut the door and looked for the page in question. In the opinion page was a piece suggesting that she was a Tecken spy and was working under Erikson's orders to gain the trust of the Council and the ISS. Once she was in the perfect position, she would overthrow the ISS and take control, as Erikson had always wanted.

"What the hell?" she blurted out.

"You didn't see that?" Zenyth said. "I thought Frederick told you to keep up with the news."

"I've been a little distracted. Besides, it's a lot to take in every day."

"Right. Anyway, I heard a rumour around the office that you'd been spotted on Tecken in the past few hours, wandering around. Which, in light of that piece, could be a very bad thing. It could give people the idea that the article's true."

"But it doesn't make sense," Kit replied. "Why would I have... done what I did to Erikson if I was on his side?"

Zenyth shrugged. "Maybe people think you're deep undercover, and it was his plan that you kill him if you needed to, to get where he couldn't. Admittedly, it's really stupid. You could have crushed the entire Cambrian Forces and marched Erikson through the Segment without breaking a sweat. And I doubt that an Erikson would ever voluntarily sacrifice themselves for the greater good."

"Those are all very good points," Kit said. Even knowing the truth, she found the article difficult to believe. It had obviously been written by someone who didn't know anything about the events of the Second Invasion, and who didn't understand that an Erikson would rather die trying to rule than sacrifice themselves to put someone else on the throne. Unfortunately that could describe most of the Segment's inhabitants.

Kit put the paper aside and crossed her arms. "If I'm supposed to bring the ISS down, why haven't I joined them yet? Why do I keep turning them down?"

"Maybe it's part of your master plan," Zenyth suggested conspiratorially. "You knew that if you went in right away that it would be too obvious. Then again," she switched back to her normal voice, "sixteen years is a long time for a bluff. Anything over ten is just wasteful. By the time you actually managed to climb your way up to the top spot of Leader, you'd be nearly seventy, and even then you'd only be the Leader of Stanton, not the rest of the Segment. And it's not like you have any offspring to hand power over to."

Kit raised an eyebrow. "Whoever wrote that article should have talked to you first. You'd have set them straight so fast their head would have spun."

Zenyth brushed the compliment off. "I don't know why the paper is bothering to publish this stuff. It's not news – it's just speculation. And, honestly, who cares anymore? No offense."

"No offense taken. I wish the world would forget about me. It'd make my life a lot easier."

"Anyway, you never answered my question. Were you on Tecken today?"

She'd been hoping that Zenyth would forget about that part, but of course she hadn't. All the distractions in the world wouldn't turn Zenyth away from her true purpose. Should she lie? Should she tell the truth?

"Well, I may have gone somewhere to clear my head…"

Zenyth groaned. "Seriously? What were you thinking?"

"I was thinking that with what's being written in the papers, and with Vaughn… I needed to go somewhere that wasn't here."

"And what's wrong with Drakkar? Or Aesira? Or any island that's not Tecken?"

Kit unconsciously took a step backwards. "I made a mistake, okay. It's not like I went over there and waved my arms around shouting *'Look at me!'* I thought that nobody would suspect me of going there, so they wouldn't think to look for me."

"Well, you were wrong, but at least it's just speculation right now." Zenyth frowned. "If anyone brings it up, lie to them. I mean, you'll have to tell Frederick the truth tomorrow, at your meeting, but don't tell anyone else."

The meeting. Kit had forgotten that tomorrow was her meeting with Frederick. She didn't want to talk to Frederick – or have anything to do with the ISS at all – but if she didn't show up, the ISS would definitely suspect something.

The phone rang, but Kit didn't move. She was so used to ignoring it that she barely noticed it, lost in her own thoughts. Zenyth waited a few rings, but when Kit didn't budge, she stood up and brushed past her.

"I guess that explains why Naydir couldn't get a hold of you," she muttered. She picked up the phone. "Hello?"

Kit only half listened to Zenyth's side of the conversation. There wasn't much to hang on to, except that something surprising must have happened. She stared off into space, wondering how she should plan her day tomorrow. She should pack her bags, go the afternoon meeting with Frederick, and then leave. It would make sense for her first stop on Tecken to be Akola's office, to talk things over. Maybe Akola wouldn't want her on

Tecken. Maybe remembering her past wouldn't be enough to make up for all she'd done. What would she do then? Where would she go?

"Kit!"

She snapped out of her fog. "What?"

Zenyth's eyes were wide as she put down the phone. "We need to go to the hospital right now. Vaughn just woke up."

CHAPTER 27

The world seemed to slow down. Kit knew that she should be jumping for joy, but was unable to move. She was happy – of course she was happy – but the truth had complicated things. Vaughn wasn't just her partner anymore, he was someone who had been assigned to watch over her by the ISS. How could she face him, knowing that her entire life had been a lie?

"New Earth to Kit," Zenyth said. "Are you there? I thought you'd be ecstatic."

"I…" Kit tried to think of a lie. "I just can't believe it. I'd almost given up hope."

"That's strangely pessimistic, but whatever. Are you ready to go?"

She tried to speak but her words came out in a flustered mess, so Zenyth grabbed her by the hand and led her out of the apartment. Kit wanted to tell her to go on without her, but it would be too suspicious if she said anything like that. Instead, she allowed herself to be brought to Zenyth's Sol-car and driven to the hospital.

"He's still a little groggy," the nurse explained, "but now that he's awake he should be feeling better soon."

Kit could only nod as she walked into the room after Zenyth. Naydir and Sav were already inside, talking to Vaughn, who was still lying in bed. The front of the bed had been propped up so that he could see them easier, but he was making no effort to lift his head. There were still bandages on his arm, but the surface area they were covering was less than before, and some of his skin merely had a red tinge to it.

"I guess I should get the name of the person who found me," he was saying to Naydir, his voice hoarse from disuse.

"You just concentrate on getting better right now," Naydir replied. "I've already thanked that person enough for all five of us."

Vaughn's head turned and he saw Zenyth and Kit. A smile broke out on his face. "We've got to stop meeting like this."

Kit's reply stuck in her throat. She knew that she should run to his side, but her feet felt heavy as she moved forward. She needed more time to reconcile the past with the present, but she couldn't do that with him lying there, looking at her like that.

When she finally made it to his side, she took his hand and managed a small smile. "Welcome back."

"I've been filling him in on what happened," Naydir said.

"Do you remember anything?" Zenyth jumped in eagerly.

Vaughn paused. "I remember getting ready to leave, because it was getting late, but then I... I think I smelled smoke. I was turning back to investigate, but then it all goes black."

Zenyth nodded, her eyes moving to the side, lost in thought.

"Did they say when you can leave?" Kit asked.

"Maybe tomorrow or the next day. There are still a few tests they want to run."

She nodded. She felt terrible because Vaughn remaining in the hospital would be more convenient for her.

"Maybe we should go and give him a chance to rest," Zenyth said. "We don't want to overwhelm him on his first day awake."

Vaughn almost laughed. "I'd like to think that I've slept enough for now. Although everything's still kind of... fuzzy."

"We'll come back tomorrow," Zenyth said. "By then you'll probably be as good as new."

"Sounds good." He looked up at Kit. "See you tomorrow?"

She smiled, making sure it reached her eyes. "Yeah. You take it easy, okay?" She gave his hand a squeeze before letting go.

"We'll be a few minutes," Naydir said, speaking for him and Sav.

Zenyth nodded and led Kit out of the room.

"Well, that's great news," Zenyth said as they walked. "He seems to be his old self, just a little groggy. And there's no memory loss." She nodded to herself. "It's really good."

"Yeah, good," Kit echoed hollowly.

"Look, I know it's hard to see him in the hospital. Probably brings up bad memories and stuff, but don't worry about it. Once he's home it'll all be fine. Trust me."

Kit felt a small wave of relief. She was worried that she'd been acting strange, but it looked like Zenyth had translated that strangeness into a logical, realistic explanation.

"Yeah, it'll all be fine once he's home," she said.

Her bag was packed and had been placed in her El-car late last night, so all she had left to do was go to her meeting with Frederick. Once this meeting was over, she could say goodbye to this fake life and hello to her real one.

Kit spend the morning practising what she'd say to Frederick. The Tecken trip would probably come up, and possibly the opinion pieces from the paper. She'd have to find some way to end the meeting quickly and get out of there without saying anything suspicious. She could do this.

When she reached the sixth floor, she greeted Teya warmly. Teya returned the greeting and then told her that she could go right in. Frederick's previous meeting had run long, but she should be along any minute. In the meantime, Kit was welcome to the refreshments inside.

Kit thanked Teya and went into Frederick's office. It was strange to be in there without the Leader, but hopefully it wouldn't be for long. First she went to the large windows and looked out over the island. In some places she could see all the way to the water. It really was a beautiful view. If this room had been on the other side of the building, she might have been able to see Tecken.

She was still standing at the window, admiring the view, when Frederick came in.

"Sorry to be late, but we were busy trying to come up with an appropriate response to that opinion piece in the paper accusing you of being a Tecken spy."

Kit was confused. "I thought you weren't going to respond to any of those?"

"Opinions are one thing, but conspiracy theories are completely different. Everyone knows that we've been trying to get you to join us for ages, so it's in our best interest to discourage that opinion. It's taking so long because we don't want to say anything that could be misconstrued." She gestured to her kitchenette. "Tea?"

"No thanks," Kit replied. She walked over to the sitting area and sat down in her usual chair, preparing herself.

Frederick poured herself a cup of tea, walked over and sat down. She took a long sip before beginning. "So, Kit, tell me all about your trip to Tecken."

She smiled after speaking, but Kit knew that she wasn't

happy.

"I'm sorry. I needed to go somewhere to clear my head. I didn't think anyone would recognize me."

"Of course not." The smile remained on Frederick's face, but her tone wasn't happy. "Why would the most famous person in the entire Segment think that anyone would recognize her? You know, your little day-trip is the reason our statement is so difficult to work out. How can we say anything when you're sneaking off to spend time on Tecken?"

"It was just the one time."

"Well, promise me that you won't go back there. We don't need this getting worse."

"I promise," she lied.

"Excellent!" Frederick took a sip of tea. "Now, what's going on that you needed to get away from?"

Her voice had gone back to sounding friendly, but Kit wasn't fooled.

"It's everything that went on with Vaughn," Kit said, almost stumbling on his name. "It brought back a lot of memories, and I needed to clear my head."

"Okay," she nodded. "Well, if there's ever anything you need to talk about, we have lots of people here who can help you. You know, you never took us up on our offer to talk to a psychiatrist after the war, but it's still standing. I know it seems that we have ulterior motives, but we really do want to help you, just like everyone else on this island."

Kit nodded politely.

"Is there anything you'd like to talk about today? Anything that you want to bring to my attention or that you need to get off your mind?"

Taking in a deep breath, Kit shook her head. "I think I just need time. These feelings will go away eventually."

Frederick raised an eyebrow. "Eventually is a pretty loaded word. It could mean two days from now or two years."

"It's just stupid stuff. And I know it's stupid, so I don't need anyone else to tell me that."

"Okay. Just as long as it's not anything serious that might cause you or anyone around you harm. It's not serious, is it?"

"No. Just a few unwanted memories." Kit wondered why Frederick had said that. What did she think was going on?

"So, there's nothing that you might want to talk to me or anyone else about?"

"No. And if we could get to the next topic, I'd much appreciate it." She was starting to get annoyed.

"All right." Frederick took another sip of tea before standing up. "I was hoping to put this off a little while longer, but I've got something to show you."

"What is it?"

"I'd rather you form your own opinions." She gestured to the door. "Let's go."

This didn't feel like a good idea, but Kit didn't know what to say. She had no idea what Frederick would want to show her, but it couldn't be good. Was it more proof linking her to Tecken? Or more stupid opinion pieces making her out to be a villain? There was no valid reason for her to decline this request, so all she could do was follow, hope for the best, and get out as soon as possible.

Rising to her feet, Kit smiled and tried to act relaxed. "Lead on."

They walked out of the office, Frederick leading the way. Teya gave them a smile as they walked past. They headed down the stairs, to the fifth floor, and over to one of the conference rooms. Frederick opened the door and gestured for Kit to go inside.

Kit wondered what she'd see she walked in. Maybe there would be a stack of papers accusing her of terrible things. Maybe it would be a large group of people accusing her of still being with Tecken. Or maybe it would be a large group of people wanting her to talk about her feelings. Hopefully it wouldn't be the last one. As if anyone on New Earth would be able to understand what she had gone through.

When she walked in, Zenyth was sitting at the table, a file folder in front of her.

"What are you doing here?" Kit asked.

She heard the door close behind her and turned around to see Frederick standing next to it.

"What's going on?" Kit said warily.

Zenyth stood up. "You're going to explain *this* to us." She opened the folder and started taking out pieces of paper, spreading them out on the table.

As Kit moved forward, she saw that they were the letters from Wes. Her mouth dropped open and her eyes widened. "How...?"

"I saw you bring something out to your car late last night, so I thought I'd do some investigating. You've been acting pretty strange lately and I wanted to keep an eye on you, in case you decided to run off or whatever. Guess I was justified in my suspicions, since you'd packed a bag and these letters. Probably hoping to make a quick get away after this meeting was done. Am I right?"

Kit didn't say anything.

"Well," Frederick said. "Is she right? Were you planning on running away to Tecken?"

"I..."

Zenyth jumped right in. "Did you actually believe that these letters were real and that you'd been born on Tecken?"

Kit crossed her arms. "I don't have to explain anything to you."

"No," Zenyth rose to her feet, her voice rising. "You need to explain *everything* to us. You need to explain why you've been acting so weird, why you've been hiding things from us, and why you were going to run away."

There was no escape. Frederick was standing by the door, blocking her exit. Suddenly Kit remembered that she was the Six-Elemental and she could take down anyone in her path. But would that be a wise thing to do? If she went crazy and started attacking people, she'd prove that she was dangerous.

"Kit, you need to realize that these letters are lies," Frederick said. "They were created to make you think that you're on Tecken's side. They're all false."

It was the exact thing that she would expect Stanton's Leader to say. She knew the truth and wouldn't be fooled any longer. She wouldn't let them mess with her mind any more than they already had.

"You actually believe that you're on their side, don't you?" Zenyth shook her head. "Kit, what did they do to you?"

"They didn't do anything but tell me the truth," she shot back.

"It's not the truth! It's all lies! Why can't you see that!?"

"You can't hold me prisoner!" Kit yelled. "I have the freedom to go where I want in this Segment, so move away from the door!" She glared at Frederick, who didn't budge.

"We're not letting you go until you've realized the truth," Frederick said, her voice steady and calm. "And I mean the *real* truth. It's too dangerous to let you out in public like this."

Kit shook her head. "No. I've spent weeks figuring out the truth, so it's too late for your lies to have any effect!" Kit called up the power of Air and shoved Frederick away from the door, before turning on Zenyth, who was already rushing towards her. Calling up Air and Ice, she summoned a stronger wind and shoved Zenyth back to the opposite wall. Zenyth hit the wall hard and fell to the floor, but Kit knew that it wouldn't keep her down for long. Grabbing the doorknob, she pulled open the door and raced into the hallway. She was almost free.

Before she could reach the stairs, she felt a sudden jolt as electricity flowed through her body. Kit dropped to the floor, breathless and stunned. When she turned to the left, she saw Naydir standing beside her, his tazer in his hand. He looked apologetic as he knelt down and brought the tazer to her side, sending electricity throughout her body again.

As the pain started to fade, Kit tried to think of which power could help her out of this situation, but before she could make a decision, Zenyth appeared in her line of vision.

"Sorry, but it needs to be done," she said, not sounding sorry at all.

The last thing Kit saw was Zenyth's fist flying towards her face.

⚡ ≈ △ □ ○ ✳

PART THREE

⚡ ≈ △ □ ○ ✳

CHAPTER 28

The weekly reports from Chief Azeil had come in, and Kendra was pleased to see that they were proving her hypothesis. Nobody on Briton knew that their newspapers were being scrutinized by other departments, so they hadn't changed their format in the slightest. The statistics of Humanist versus Elemental crimes had become so lop-sided that it was almost impossible to chart.

After completing her elemental training, Kendra had moved to Stanton to work with the ISS. Pitor hadn't been happy about the change of plan, but she made it clear that this was the best way to achieve their goal. Besides, it wasn't like she was going to give up and go back to Tecken, just because Pitor wanted her to. She wasn't six years old anymore.

Even though she'd only worked for the ISS for a couple of months, she'd already made great strides, bringing attention to what was happening on Briton. Aside from wanting to take down the Humanists as soon as possible, she knew that something like this could really help her career.

As she finished reading Azeil's reports, she couldn't help thinking how easy it had been to convince the ISS to investigate this matter. When she first started working, she noticed that the ISS had newspapers from all over the Segment delivered.

The employees were encouraged to read them, but most people stuck to the *Stanton News*. Occasionally papers from Drakkar, Aesira, and Cambria would be read by employees missing their home island, and some people would read the Tecken paper once in a while – to keep an eye on what was going on over there – but it was rare for the Briton paper to be picked up.

She began taking the *Briton Truth* with her and reading it around the office. After a few days the right person noticed what she was reading and commented on it. She casually mentioned how she'd studied on Briton for a year and had noticed a strange formula to their crime pages and was checking to see if it was still there.

That original passing comment had turned into an hour-long conversation, where she filled him in on all the strange things she'd noticed about Briton. She may have played a little dumber than normal, but she wanted him to come to his own conclusions. It worked, and the next thing she knew, the both of them were in the office of Ren Wyck, the Segment liaison, telling him about their concerns.

From there it had moved slower than Kendra would have liked, but she understood the need for discretion. Wyck wanted to make sure that they weren't reading too much into this, so he assigned a task to the Stanton Police to study all of the Segment's newspapers, hoping that others might come to the same conclusion. He'd also mentioned it to the liaisons on Cambria, Drakkar, Aesira, and Tecken so that they could do the same experiment if they wished.

When the initial findings came in, Kendra was pleased that others had discovered the same strange pattern, although she was a little disappointed that it had only been two of Stanton's officers. She'd hoped that it would be obvious to everyone and that the reports would come flying in, but then had to remind herself that it had been the lack of interest from other islands that had allowed the Humanists to flourish in the first place. One of the best parts of this experiment was that one officer had gone above and beyond what was expected by writing a ten-page report on her findings. Kendra had read the report and was thoroughly impressed. It had some really good ideas in it, which she was sure the ISS would use. She was surprised to see that it had been written by Zenyth Hansen, a friend of Tyler's, but she still had to admire the effort. Maybe Hansen would be a good ally to have.

Wyck had given their findings to the other Segment liaisons, and now they were waiting to hear back. In the meantime, they were crafting a plan to figure out why there seemed to be no non-Elemental crime on Briton.

Kendra had been put on this team and she knew that she was lucky to be there. Even though this had started because of her observation, she was still a brand new employee. They could have given her a thank-you and moved ahead with more senior employees, but instead they asked her if she wanted to be involved. She accepted immediately.

So far she was proving herself to be a great addition, making helpful suggestions, but being sure not to overstep her bounds. She couldn't wait until the ISS's first ever Officer Exchange Program was finalized and they were able to take a large step towards making Briton a safer place for Elementals.

"Have you heard the news?"

Kendra looked up from the report. Rae was standing near her desk, her orange eyes wide with disbelief.

"About what?"

Rae pulled up a chair and sat down next to her. She leaned in close and lowered her voice. "Apparently the Six-Elemental is currently in custody. In the basement."

Kendra's eyes widened. "Seriously?"

Rae nodded.

"Why is she in custody? What happened?"

"I heard a rumour that she snapped and thinks she's back on Tecken's side. Frederick and a few others confronted her yesterday and she went berserk."

"Wow..." Kendra shook her head. "That's crazy. And she's here? In the basement? The ISS hasn't used those holding cells since the war..."

"I know, but where else would you keep the most powerful person on the Segment?"

"What do you think they're going to do with her?"

Rae shrugged. "Probably the same thing they did last time she thought she was on Tecken's side. Try to make her realize the truth. Anyway, I should mention to you that this is all just rumour and that it probably shouldn't be spread around, but I heard it from four other people this morning, so obviously it's not going to stay secret for long. I wouldn't be surprised if it was in the paper tomorrow."

Her pessimism made Kendra laugh. "Something this big wouldn't stay secret for long. Especially after that rumour about her being spotted on Tecken."

"Oh yeah. The timing of this is insane."

"Thanks for giving me a heads up. I'll try to act surprised if anyone else mentions it."

Rae smiled. "No problem. Have fun reading all your reports."

Rae headed back to her desk in the Community Matters Department, where Kendra had worked before moving to the Briton project. In the short time she'd been there, they'd become friends, and Kendra had to admit that it was helpful knowing someone who found out all of the good gossip early.

The news about the Six-Elemental brought a smile to Kendra's lips. The basement of the ISS had been used as holding rooms for Tecken spies after the First Invasion and again after the Second Invasion, but there had been no need for it once Tecken had been peacefully integrated back into the Segment. Until now.

It was too perfect. Once rumour spread that the Six-Elemental was being held down there, the world would finally realize that she was more of a liability than an asset.

CHAPTER 29

"It's not working," Naydir sighed. He was tired and frustrated, and out of ideas. When they'd had to restore Kit's memories during the Second Invasion, it had been surprisingly easy. Zenyth and he had brought up a number of specific past memories and within minutes she was back with them. This time, however, nothing was getting through to her. She thought that everything they said was a lie fabricated by the ISS, meant to keep her under their thumb. It was almost as if she didn't want to remember.

"It's those stupid letters," Zenyth grumbled, sitting down next to him on the bench. "They told her not to trust us, so she refuses to believe anything we say. She thinks that we're trying to trick her."

They were in the hallway of the ISS's basement, a few doors down from the room where Kit was being held. A guard was scheduled to stand outside the door at all times, which had made conversing awkward at first, but then Zenyth stopped caring about what the guards heard. Why would they be here if they hadn't been proven trustworthy? Although it would have been nice if they'd offer up some helpful ideas instead of just standing there, watching the door.

"But why does she believe those letters?" Naydir asked. "I

mean, she must remember her real past. She lived it, after all."

Zenyth shrugged. "I have no idea what's going on inside her head. Maybe when Tecken brainwashed her the first time they added this secondary back-up brainwashing thing, and those letters brought it out." She sighed. "And you have to admit that this current situation isn't giving us any brownie points."

After Naydir had tazed Kit to stop her from running away, and Zenyth knocked her out, they'd brought her down to one of the holding rooms in the basement of the ISS building. The rooms had been maintained, just in case they were needed sometime in the future, which made Zenyth wonder if the ISS had been preparing for this kind of thing. Not only were they holding her in a room normally reserved for Tecken spies, they had also restrained her power with an Element-cancelling collar – the same design that Tecken had used on her sixteen years ago. Whenever Zenyth tried to look at the situation from Kit's point of view, she couldn't deny that everyone involved with the ISS looked like the bad guys.

"Have we decided who's telling Vaughn yet?" she asked.

Naydir shook his head. "Are you volunteering?"

"You know that he's going to want to go in there."

"I know. We need to keep him away as long as possible."

They sat in silence for a few seconds, staring at the dark grey walls. The lighting in the hallway was harsh, and after spending so much time down here, Zenyth now considered the holding cells in the police station to be positively radiating with warmth.

The room where Kit was being held wasn't a bad room, but it wasn't the best. The bed, which was the only furniture in the room, was fairly comfortable and there was a private bathroom area. They were trying to be nice to her while also restraining her, which was a difficult line to walk.

Frederick was depending on the two of them to bring Kit out of whatever mental state she was in, but nothing they'd done so far had worked. They'd tried talking to her and bringing in specialists to talk to her, but Kit wouldn't trust anyone. In her eyes, everyone was an ISS spy.

Zenyth had read over all of the letters they'd found in Kit's possession, but she didn't know what to do about them. They'd tried showing Kit that the ISS reports were fakes, comparing them to official ISS reports from that time and pointing out the subtle differences in the logo and ink colour, but it achieved nothing. Whatever rabbit hole her brain had fallen into, it was going to take a lot more to get it out.

They'd put off telling Vaughn, hoping that they'd be able to bring Kit back before he was released from the hospital, but he was leaving today and there was still no light at the end of the tunnel. Zenyth knew that he'd want to come here, but she doubted that it would help. She'd seen how Kit had reacted to Vaughn after he'd come out of his coma and knew that her suspicions had spread to him as well. It was that exact moment when Zenyth knew that something was terribly, horribly wrong.

Seeing Kit like this would break Vaughn's heart, and Zenyth didn't want that to happen.

"I'll tell him," she sighed.

"Really?"

"Yeah. I'll probably have to strong-arm him to stop him from coming here, but we can't let him see her. Not like this."

"Agreed."

They sat in silence for another minute. Finally, Zenyth rose to her feet.

"Well, I'd better get going. See you later?"

Naydir nodded sadly. "See you later."

≈

During the drive home from the hospital, Zenyth managed to dodge the majority of Vaughn's questions. She tried to distract him by asking about his health and what he was and wasn't allowed to do now that he was out of the hospital. She already knew the answers to those questions because she'd arrived early to speak to the doctors, but it was the only topic of conversation she could think of. As Vaughn answered her questions, she tried to figure out if he was stable enough to handle the terrible information that was coming.

When they reached his apartment, he called out for Kit, but there was no answer. Zenyth took in a deep, steadying breath and closed the door behind them.

"Vaughn, let's sit in the living room for a minute."

He looked confused, but then some kind of realization sank in. "What's wrong with her?"

"Sit first. And yes, it's that bad."

Obediently, he walked into the living room and sat down on the couch, bracing himself.

Zenyth filled him in on what was happening, trying to be as tactful as possible while also trying to convey the utter feeling of hopelessness. To his credit, he didn't fight her on anything. When she finished talking, she waited for him to say something.

"I thought she was acting strange at the hospital," he said quietly.

"Yeah, I picked up on that, too."

He frowned. "She really thinks that we're all spies, keeping an eye on her for the ISS?"

She nodded. "We don't know what to do. We've tried everything, but she doesn't trust any of us."

"What if I—"

"No!" Zenyth jumped right in. "Remember the hospital? You're in the group of untrustworthy people, just like my brother and I. Your talking to her won't change anything."

Vaughn's frown deepened. "So, what do we do?"

He sounded utterly defeated. Zenyth wanted nothing more than to say something reassuring, but she had no words.

□

Naydir was wracking his brain, trying to think of a different tactic they could try, but every idea he came up with seemed stupid and pointless. If trained psychologists couldn't help her, what could he hope to do? He needed Kit to trust him, but how? She saw everything he did as an ISS tactic, instead of a genuine concern for her wellbeing.

If they didn't find a way to get Kit back to her old self soon, then the ISS would label her a hopeless cause and probably leave her in the basement forever. As hopeless as he felt, he couldn't give up.

Taking in a deep breath, he walked down to Kit's room. Looking through the peephole, he saw that she was sitting on the bed, staring at the wall. He knocked on the door.

"It's Naydir."

She didn't respond. Her only reaction was to cross her arms over her chest.

He unlocked the door and walked inside. "I have a few questions I'd like to ask you. You don't have to answer them now, but I'd appreciate it if you'd at least think about them."

There was no reply, but at least she hadn't told him to shut up.

"Question one: do you really think that the ISS would be able to kidnap one of the most important people on Tecken and remove her from the island without anyone noticing? Question two: why would the ISS brainwash you to know that you're the

Six-Elemental, but want you to keep it secret? And question three: concerning your elemental Vision, you told us that when you received your Vision it was so intense that you blacked out, but when you were with Tecken you thought that it was nothing more special than a normal Vision. So why would the ISS go to the trouble of creating this strange Vision for you instead of going with something more normal?"

She said nothing.

He held back a sigh. "Can you promise me that you'll at least think about these?"

She glared at him. "Why should I promise you anything? You're holding me here against my will, and you've taken away my powers. I don't owe you a thing."

"We've taken your powers away because you could level this building and everyone in it," he explained gently. "I know how terrible you felt after the Second Invasion when you learned how many people had been hurt because of you, so when you finally realize the truth, I wouldn't want anything like that on your conscience."

"I've already realized the truth," she shot back. "No matter how many times you say I'm wrong, I won't forget it. Not again. One day you'll realize that you've made a terrible mistake in keeping me here like this."

He shook his head. "Just promise me that you'll think about those questions, okay?" He turned to exit the room.

"I've already thought about them."

He looked back and saw that Kit had risen to her feet. She didn't move forward, but her body language radiated power and anger.

"Answer number one: yes. I wouldn't put anything past the ISS. There were multiple spies living on Tecken who could have accomplished such a thing. Answer number two: of course they'd want me to hide my powers. They couldn't exactly parade me around in front of everyone and hope that Tecken wouldn't find out where I was. And answer number three: I don't care. You're clutching at straws because you know that you have nothing."

Any hope he'd entered the room with was gone and Naydir left without another word. Once he was back in the hallway, he sat on the bench and put his head in his hands. It was starting to feel like the more they tried, the worse it got. The more persuasive they were, the more stubborn she became.

He would have given anything to have the old Kit back, but he didn't know if she still existed.

≈

Vaughn had gone to bed hours ago, but Zenyth was having trouble sleeping. Although Vaughn hadn't looked pleased when she informed him that she'd be spending the night on his couch, he hadn't told her to go away. She was worried about leaving him alone, considering that he'd just gotten out of the hospital *and* had a major bombshell dropped on him. Sleeping on a couch would be worth it if he made it through the night without any trouble.

The news of Kit had hit him hard. In fact, Zenyth wouldn't have been surprised if Vaughn was still awake, lying in bed, trying to think of some way to help Kit. If that were the case, at least he was being quiet about it.

She knew that there had to be some solution that they hadn't thought of yet. They'd already done everything they could to convince her that she was from Briton, short of bringing in her family. Everyone had agreed that bringing in her mother and step-father wouldn't help, just like nothing would be achieved by bringing in Bryanna or Cale, but Zenyth was almost ready to jump to those last resorts. Maybe seeing her step-father and remembering all the arguments she'd had with him would jog Kit's memory. Or maybe it would strengthen her resolve to believe that her past on Briton had been a lie.

If only they knew who had written those letters. It had to be someone from Tecken, but the author had covered their tracks extremely well. There were no fingerprints or clues for them to follow, and they couldn't go around accusing people without proof. Zenyth started pacing around the living room, hoping that the action would tire her. As much as she wanted to go to sleep, she couldn't turn her brain off. There had to be an answer out there, somewhere – some angle or idea that they hadn't considered yet.

Suddenly an idea popped into her head. They'd spent the past couple of days trying to convince Kit that she was from Briton, but they hadn't really tried to convince her that she *wasn't* from Tecken. A plan started to form. It wasn't the best plan ever created, and she didn't know if she'd be able to get the help she needed, but if it worked it might bring an end to this.

CHAPTER 30

"You work too much."

Kendra laughed at the statement, but she knew it was true. "Well, I've got a very big project going on. Maybe I'll have more free time in the future."

Skye shook her head. "*Maybe* is not the answer I was looking for. Normally I expect my best friend to not be such a hard worker, but I've given up hope in you a long time ago, you *public servant.*"

They were having supper at Slice & Dice, a restaurant downtown that was Skye-approved. When she first moved back to Stanton, Kendra had been worried that her former roommate would be too busy hanging out with newer friends and wouldn't have time for her, but Skye had been delighted to learn that Kendra was back on the island permanently. When they met up, it was like no time had passed since they last saw each other.

While Kendra was busy exploring the Segment, Skye had finally chosen a major, stuck with it, and graduated. She was still in university, however this time she was the teacher. When Kendra learned this, she remarked that Skye could probably teach every single course being offered, due to her many years jumping between classes. Instead of being bashful, Skye agreed with her.

"I apologize for being so good at my job." Kendra tried to lay on the charm, but she knew that Skye would require more appeasement than that.

"Oh, did you hear the latest rumour?"

Kendra shook her head, thankful that Skye was so easily distracted. "You know I don't pay attention to rumours, but do go on."

Skye leaned forward and lowered her voice. "Apparently the Six-Elemental's gone crazy and thinks that she's a Tecken spy."

"Seriously?" Kendra replied, acting as if this was the first time she'd heard such a thing.

"Yeah. Apparently the ISS are holding her in their cells – the ones they haven't used since the Second Invasion. I'm surprised you haven't heard this."

"I'd heard a rumour about the basement holding cells being used again, but I had no idea what it was for. Do you think it's true?"

Skye nodded. "Tyler was spotted on Tecken a few days ago, so I'd believe it. I think all those letters in the newspapers have pushed her over the edge."

"After some of the stuff I read, I wouldn't be surprised. Whoever's writing that stuff really has an issue with the Six-Elemental."

"It's probably some crazy Humanists from Briton." Skye looked at her watch. "The movie starts soon, we should hurry up and finish."

"Only if you promise to stop making fun of my work ethic," Kendra teased.

Skye rolled her eyes. "You know I can't do that."

Δ

When Kendra decided to work for the ISS on Stanton instead of Tecken, she knew that strategically it would be a better way to endear herself to the people of the Segment. Despite the ISS's attempts at integration, most people from Tecken didn't leave the island, or if they left for university, they returned soon after graduating. Not many people moved to Tecken, so at least it wasn't a one-sided argument. Kendra wanted to prove that people from Tecken were just as conscientious about issues on other islands, and shatter people's pre-conceived notions.

However, she wasn't ready to tell everyone that she was from Tecken just yet. Although the higher-ups in the ISS knew, she'd held that particular piece of information back from her co-workers, wanting them to form their own opinions about her first. Maybe once the Briton task force was in play, she'd let people know. Or maybe after that.

The only problem with that plan was that she really wanted to tell Skye the truth. The more time they spent together, the more she wanted to let Skye know who she really was. She valued their friendship and didn't want to continue lying by omission. Hopefully Skye wouldn't have an issue with it, but there was always a possibility, which is why it would be better for Kendra to tell the truth sooner rather than later.

When the movie finished, they went for a walk downtown to discuss what they'd thought about it. They usually agreed overall, but there were always some small parts that they would argue about. Kendra didn't know why, but she enjoyed arguing with Skye. Maybe it was because nothing they argued about was really serious, so the stakes weren't high. It didn't matter who was right and who was wrong, as long as they were spending time together.

"Fine," Skye sighed. "I will acknowledge that the lighting

was really good in the end scene and not overly trite."

Kendra held back her laughter. "As much as I enjoy this victory, I have something I need to talk to you about."

Skye paused. "I... um, is this..." She paused again. "Because I have something I wanted to tell you, too, and I think it might be the same thing."

"You do?" Kendra couldn't have been more confused if Skye was speaking a different language.

"Yeah. I mean, I think it's time for certain things to be said out in the open."

It was Kendra's turn to pause. "What are you talking about?"

"Huh?"

"What do you think I want to say?"

Skye shrugged. "I don't know. I mean, we hang out a lot and stuff, and I really enjoy spending time with you and care about you, and I don't think I'm alone in that. Right?"

Kendra felt her cheeks heating up as she finally realized what Skye was saying. "Oh. Um, I need you to put a pin in that for a moment. But we'll definitely come back to it. It's just that I should really say my thing first."

Skye motioned for her to continue.

Kendra took a deep breath and let it out slowly. "I know I don't talk much about my past, but I just wanted you to know that I'm not from Drakkar, as I may have implied. I was actually born on Tecken. I wanted to get out and explore the rest of the Segment, because I know that there's more out there than what we were told growing up. I know I never said anything about it, but there's a lot of history between these two islands, and I thought it would be best if I avoided the subject, and, well, I just want to make sure that you knew the truth, now, before..."

She looked over at Skye, who looked confused, as if she was

trying to process the information but was having a hard time trying to make it fit. Kendra looked down at her feet, unsure if she should say more or stay quiet. At least she'd finally said it.

"Um," Skye said slowly. "Well, I was not expecting that."

"I'm sorry."

"Like, I know you were young when the Second Invasion happened, so it's not like it was your fault. I'm just surprised that you kept this from me."

Kendra shrugged, embarrassed. "I wanted to make sure you either liked or hated me because of my personality and not my home island. Most people's reaction is instant hate, and I wanted you to get to know the actual me. If it makes you feel better, you're the first person I've told. Well, other than my bosses."

Skye thought about it. "Okay, that does make me feel a little better." She sat down on a nearby bench. "I mean, I want to say that I'd have been a bigger person and wouldn't have let that affect what I thought about you, but I really don't know. I've grown up knowing what the Eriksons have done to Tecken and Stanton, so I'm sure that would have coloured my opinion, even in some small way. So, even if I wanted to be mad that you kept this from me, I don't know if I can."

The response was good, but Kendra could tell that Skye was still having trouble processing the information. "If you need some time to think this over, I can go."

"No. It shouldn't change anything." Skye stood up, a determined look on her face. "You're still you. The person you were when you were six isn't the person you are now. And I know who you really are. Unless you're holding more information back from me..." she narrowed her eyes.

Kendra's brain rifled through the rest of her secrets. Magnus Erikson being her biological father was a pretty big deal, but when she thought about it, she wasn't actually an Erikson.

Magnus had nothing to do with her childhood, her life, nor her path right now. Her achievements were her own, not his, and she would succeed because she was the best person for the job, not because of her EDNA.

Smiling, Kendra shook her head. "I can't think of anything else."

Skye sighed again. "Well, then I guess we should probably continue as normal."

She smiled. "That would be great."

They continued on their walk, but Kendra could tell that her earlier revelation was still on Skye's mind. Maybe it had been the wrong time to bring it up. Maybe once Skye had time to process it, she'd realize that she couldn't look past it and they'd never be friends again.

When it came time for them to split off in their own directions – Skye towards her apartment building in the East and Kendra towards hers at the ISS apartment buildings – Kendra wasn't sure what to say. She wanted to apologize again, but before she could, Sky spoke.

"It's stupid, you know?"

"What?" Kendra asked, confused.

"To blame people for something that they had no hand in. To be prejudiced towards someone who doesn't deserve it. Your being from Tecken shouldn't change anything that I feel towards you. If anything, I should acknowledge that growing up there is what made you the way you are – the lame public servant who wants to help everyone in the Segment."

Kendra couldn't help smiling. "Thank you..?"

Skye reached out and took her hand, giving it a squeeze. "And even though I think that public servants are the worst, I like you Kendra. I really do."

"I really like you, too, Skye." The smile spread wider on

her face.

"Would you like to come back to my place, so we can talk some more?"

"I'd love to."

CHAPTER 31

There was 'uncomfortable' and then there was *'Why did I come here? This is the stupidest idea I've ever had in my entire life'* uncomfortable. Zenyth was currently experiencing the second feeling and not liking it at all. She hadn't told anyone else what she was doing because she didn't know if they'd agree with it and she wasn't prepared to back down. All she'd said to Naydir and Vaughn was that she had something to do and would be back in a couple hours.

"You can go in now," the receptionist smiled, putting more friendliness into her inflection than was normally called for. Zenyth had a feeling that the receptionist was overcompensating, but she had presented herself as an officer of Stanton and hadn't explained why she was here, trying to get an audience with Tecken's Leader without an appointment.

Zenyth stood up, straightened her shirt, and thanked the receptionist as she walked through the door. She'd been expecting an office like Frederick's, but it was quite different. It was the same size and had windows along three of the walls, but the rest of the design was more function than form. Filing cabinets lined the fourth wall, and there was no kitchenette or no place to sit down, except for two chairs across from a large desk.

Sitting behind the desk was Akola Allen, the Leader of

Tecken. Aside from being an incredible soldier, she had been in the room when Erikson died and had taken command of the island before the Second Invasion even ended.

Zenyth hadn't had much contact with her, but she knew from Kit's stories that Akola had been Kit's best friend while she'd been on Tecken and had been in charge of watching her and making sure the reassignment didn't fail. She knew that Akola was an Earth Elemental, and that her actual hair was blonde, but she dyed it bright red in order to seem more Elemental. Other than that, she knew that Akola could be tough as nails and difficult to work with.

"Good morning, Officer Hansen," Akola said, not bothering to stand. "Would you care to take a seat?"

"Good morning, Leader Allen," Zenyth said politely, sitting in one of the chairs. "I have a somewhat sensitive matter to discuss with you."

Akola gave her the once-over. "I know that you're friends with Katherine Tyler, that you were on the ISS's civilian team, and you fought in the Second Invasion. I bring this up because I know who you are. If you're here on your own and not on a special assignment from the ISS or the police, then I've already assumed the reason. Gossip travels fast."

Zenyth reminded herself that she was here to ask a favour, so she shouldn't react to Akola's hostility.

"Well, then. Here's the deal." She took in a breath and let it out in a huff. "Someone's been mailing Kit strange letters, trying to convince her that she's actually from Tecken and that Stanton brainwashed her first. Turns out that Kit's started to believe it all, and we can't convince her otherwise. So, I was hoping that you'd be kind enough to go to Stanton and tell Kit the truth."

Akola raised an eyebrow. "Well, I had not been expecting that last bit."

"Yeah, it's a bit of a shocker."

Akola took a moment to think, so Zenyth sat quietly. She still wasn't sure if coming here was a mistake or not, but Akola seemed to be a level-headed person. Hopefully her hatred for Kit wasn't as strong as her sense of duty.

"Other than good community relations, why should I help the ISS? What can I possibly do that you can't?"

Zenyth shrugged. "We've tried everything else. The only thing we haven't tried is to get someone who grew up on Tecken to tell her that it's all a load of lies. Honestly, if you can't get through to her, then I'm officially out of ideas. And as for the 'why should you help us?' Well, if Kit truly believes she's from Tecken then she'll want to move out here, so she'll become your problem, not ours."

It felt mean to say, but it was true.

After a much longer time than Zenyth had patience for, Akola finally nodded.

"Fine, I'll help you. I'll rearrange a few things in today's schedule, but don't expect me to stay on Stanton for long. There are other matters that require my attention."

"Hey, I'll take what I can get." Zenyth rose to her feet. "So... When do you think you'll be able to make it over?"

She shuffled through a few pages on her desk. "Would early afternoon work? I'd appreciate some time to prepare myself."

"Afternoon is fine. Thank you. I really appreciate it."

Akola nodded at her, and Zenyth exited the room. She gave a polite nod to the receptionist before heading out of the building. Now all that was left was for her to go back to Stanton and tell everyone what she'd done.

≈

Naydir was in the lunch room, talking with Sav, when Zenyth arrived back on Stanton.

"Where'd you go?" Naydir asked. "I had to tell Frederick that you were working on a secret plan that was so secret even I didn't know what it was."

"Um…" She had spent the entire drive over thinking of how to phrase her impromptu road-trip, but she still had nothing. "I was exploring alternate options…?"

Sav frowned. "I have a feeling that this conversation should be happening somewhere more private."

Zenyth nodded. "That might be an accurate feeling."

The three of them headed towards the basement, trying to look as inconspicuous and uninteresting as possible. They knew that rumours were spreading around the island, but they didn't want to do anything to feed into them. Some people thought that the ISS was working on a way to give people elemental powers and had kidnapped Kit to get her EDNA, others thought that the Six-Elemental was sick or dying and had been brought here to keep it quiet, while others were much closer – suspecting that the Six-Elemental had finally outed herself as a Tecken spy and had been contained by the ISS before she could destroy Stanton.

As much as Zenyth wanted to correct these rumours, she held her tongue. The truth wouldn't help right now.

They no longer had to flash their clearance badges to the guard standing beside the door to the basement, since everyone scheduled for this particular security job knew their faces. The guard nodded at them and unlocked the entrance.

"So, what did you do?" Naydir asked as soon as they were in the basement.

"I went to speak to Akola Allen."

Both Naydir and Sav stared at her.

"And did she kick you out?" Sav finally asked.

Zenyth shook her head. "I told her what was going on and

asked if she could help. I figured that Kit would believe the truth if she heard it from someone who actually lived on Tecken."

Naydir let out a breath. "That's a very rational thought, but I wish you'd discussed it with one of us beforehand. What if Frederick had already thought about that and decided not to pursue it?"

"After what Kit did, I doubt that anyone would want to ask Tecken for help – especially Frederick. I only went because I didn't know what else to do." She looked towards the room where Kit was behind held. "Akola will be here this afternoon. If she fails, well, then I'm officially out of ideas."

Naydir and Sav followed her gaze.

"Me too," Naydir said quietly.

It didn't have to be said out loud, but they all knew that time was running out.

CHAPTER 32

The situation felt familiar, but Kit wasn't sure why. There had been another room, in the past, and a collar that took her powers away, but the other details were hazy. She couldn't trust her memory anymore, so she tried not to think about the past and focus on the present.

Her hand reached up to touch the collar around her neck. She hated this thing more than she could describe. Words hadn't been invented yet that could communicate what she was feeling. Whenever she tried to use one of her powers, the collar stopped her, making it difficult for her to concentrate. She would have loved to rip it off, but they informed her that the collar had a large needle at the back that went into her neck, and unless it was removed properly, she could do permanent damage to herself.

There was nothing in the room other than the bed, so she had plenty of time to think about how the ISS was only proving her suspicions. They were trying to treat her well, apologizing for locking her up and making sure she was well fed, but she could see through their act. Every day was filled with people wanting to talk to her and trick her. She was surprised that they hadn't brought someone in to brainwash her again. Maybe that would happen today.

She'd already considered trying to escape, but she wouldn't get far with this stupid collar. Even if she managed to incapacitate the person coming in, she'd still have to face any guards in the basement, and then anyone else from that point on. She had no idea how many people were guarding her room, but it was probably a lot.

Maybe she should pretend to be on their side, make them think that they'd finally gotten through to her, and that everything was back to being perfect. She'd only have to pretend until the collar was gone. Would she be able to fool them? Would it work? Or would they leave her to die down here?

A knock on the door brought her back to reality.

"It's Zenyth. I'm coming in."

Kit sighed to herself and turned away from the door. She needed time to come up with a plan, but she'd never get that as long as the ISS continued to bother her.

"You've got a visitor," Zenyth told her. "I thought I'd give you a heads up, because it's probably not anyone you're expecting to see."

That was intriguing enough to earn Kit's attention. "Who is it?"

"Don't worry. You'll recognize her."

A woman with bright red hair and green eyes walked in. Kit's eyes widened as a flood of memories washed over her.

"Akola?"

She nodded, crossing her arms. "I didn't want to come here, but I heard that you'd found yourself in some trouble."

"Oh," Kit said flatly. "They got to you, too."

Zenyth started to speak, but Akola raised her hand to interrupt her.

"Maybe you should leave us."

"No way," Zenyth protested. "I'm not leaving you alone

with her."

Akola raised an eyebrow. "All of a sudden you don't trust me?"

Zenyth opened her mouth before shutting it again. "Um..." She looked from Akola to Kit. It suddenly became apparent that it would be extremely stupid to leave the two of them alone. What if Akola decided that it would be worth the hassle to have the Six-Elemental on Tecken's side and confirmed everything Kit thought? What if she demanded that Kit be allowed to leave with her? What if this idea was actually a terrible mistake?

"I want to speak to Akola alone," Kit spoke up. "If you don't leave, I won't say a damn word."

Letting out a sigh, Zenyth knew that she had lost the fight. She had to trust that the Tecken Leader would tell the truth.

"Fine," Zenyth said, trying not to scowl.

Once she was out of the room, Kit turned to Akola. "Are you working for them?"

Akola laughed bitterly. "Of course not."

"So I can trust you?"

She paused and took a long look at the blue-haired woman in front of her. "You know, I almost didn't believe Zenyth, but I'm glad I got to see this for myself. Kit Tyler, back under Tecken's control." She laughed again. "Are you as naive as last time, or was that all a show for Magnus?"

Kit rose to her feet. "I know who I truly am right now, so you can save your condescension. And, honestly, why should you be angry with me when it was the ISS who brainwashed me to kill Erikson? I wasn't myself, so you can't blame that on me. Not anymore."

Akola took a step back. "Wow... Whoever did this to you really did a number. You actually believe it? That you were born on Tecken and that your life on Briton was a lie?" Her voice dropped to a whisper. "If Wes had known about this technique, we might have actually won the war..."

"You know, as the Leader of Tecken, you can demand that they let me go. I have just as much right as anyone else to live wherever I want." Kit didn't know why she was trying to reason with Akola. It was becoming apparent that she couldn't trust her any more than the others.

Akola shook her head. "You're not from Tecken, Kit. You'd never set foot on the place until we brought you over before the Second Invasion."

"Lies."

"Fine. If you're from Tecken, tell me this: what was Magnus Erikson's coronation like?"

Kit opened her mouth to speak but then closed it again. "I don't remember. The ISS destroyed all of my memories."

"That's weird. Because even though I was young when Magnus came to power, I still remember every single moment of that day. I doubt that anything could be done to me that would make me forget it." She snapped her fingers. "I know, how about I give you some details and see if it jogs your memory? Do you remember his entrance on the balcony? What about his first speech as Leader? How about the funeral for his mother that we held just hours beforehand?"

Sitting down, Kit tried to conjure up any kind of memory of this day, but there was nothing. She tried to put Erikson on a balcony, but she couldn't remember what he looked like as a young man. She didn't even know what balcony Akola was talking about. And who had his mother been?

"The ISS—"

"Stop going on about the ISS! If they'd destroyed your memories so completely, how do you know for sure that you grew up on Tecken?"

This question put some fire back into Kit's spirit. "I know because I found my childhood home and talked to my mother."

Her answer surprised Akola. "Your mother? I don't know who you talked to or what they said to you, but that person wasn't your mother."

"And how would you know that?"

"Because I've lived on Tecken my entire life," she said, her voice rising with anger. "Because I have been responsible for every soul on that island for the past sixteen years, after you murdered their leader. So you'd better believe me when I tell you that the person pretending to be your mother was lying, because I know everyone who lives on Tecken, and she isn't one of them."

There was something about her anger that rang true, and Kit had to sit back down on the bed. Her formerly unshakeable confidence was wavering. What would Akola have to gain by lying to her?

Akola frowned and looked down at her. "I'm sure you can remember what it like when you trained with us on Stanton, so how about I bring up a few small points that might help you make up your mind? One: if you had been born on Tecken, why didn't you have a weapon to train with? We all had one. We all trained with weapons the first year we entered the army. Why were you, a person who hadn't yet become the Six-Elemental, so important that you could get away with having no weapons training at all? Two: why were you so far behind us in fighting skill? Everyone on Tecken had to take mandatory army training for two years, so why did the rest of us have to lower our skill to make you feel better every time we trained with you? Three: why didn't they let you go and see your supposed mother once we were back on the island? Why did they keep you isolated when they knew full well that it might be your last chance to talk to her? Or why didn't they bring her in to see you and strengthen your ties to the island? Four: why couldn't you see Nathan for the asshole that he was? If you'd grown up with us, you'd have seen how terrible he acted after he didn't get an element on his twenty-first birthday, and you'd have known to stay the hell away. And, finally, five: if you were really born on Tecken, why don't you feel that overwhelming pride towards your island or a strong desire to make the world a better place? Why are you so content to spend the rest of your life hiding away, instead of working with the ISS to improve relations with Tecken or Briton? Why isn't there some small part of you that wants to help the people of this Segment instead of resenting them for being in awe of you – something that they can't help, because you're an actual myth come to life!?" She was almost shouting by this point, so she paused to bring her voice back down. "You are not from Tecken, Kit. Get it through your thick skull and stop tormenting everyone around you. And go see a psychiatrist. You obviously need one."

She started to move towards the door, but Kit called out to her.

"Wait!" She rose to her feet again. Her voice was shaking, but there was still a small bit of resolve left. "How do I know that I can trust you? How do I know that you're not lying?"

Akola walked back, stopping a few inches away from Kit's face. Her eyes burned with rage.

"Because I hate you, Kit. Because it would give me so much pleasure to sneak in here under the pretence that I'm working with the ISS just to tell you that, yes, you actually are from Tecken. I would love to see you crumble with the realization that you ruined the lives of everyone you once swore to protect, and that you murdered the most beloved man on that island and destroyed everything that he worked for. But I'm not a liar. You're not from Tecken. You never were and you never will be, so stay on Stanton with the ISS, because that's where you've always belonged, even if you're too stupid to figure it out."

Kit's eyes widened with shock. She felt as if she might throw up. No, it couldn't be true. If everything in those letters was a lie, then she'd put her friends through hell for nothing.

Akola took a deep breath and looked off to the side. "I loved him, you know," she said, her voice suddenly full of emotion. She turned back to Kit. "Not just as a Leader – not in the way that others said they did. I loved that man with all of my heart. And I watched him die – I watched you kill him. So believe me when I say that if you had been under the control of the ISS, I probably could have forgiven you. But you weren't. You murdered him, in cold blood, under no one's control but your own."

She turned and walked out of the room without another word.

Once Akola was gone, Kit's last bit of self-control evaporated. Her legs buckled underneath her, and she dropped to the floor.

CHAPTER 33

Akola stormed out the room, her face a mix of anger and sadness and frustration. She stopped near Zenyth, Naydir, and Sav, taking a moment to compose herself, but didn't make eye contact with any of them.

"If that didn't work, then I don't know what will. But I'm done."

With those words, she marched out of the hallway. Nobody tried to stop her.

Zenyth moved to the door and looked through the peephole. Kit was on the floor, huddled into a ball. She couldn't see Kit's face, but from the way her body was trembling, Zenyth had a feeling that Akola's talk had done its job. The only question was whether or not Kit had enough sanity left to survive the truth.

≈

After waiting a few minutes, Zenyth went back to the door to check on Kit. She was still on the floor, but had stopped shaking. Her back was to the door and her head bowed low.

Zenyth knocked and announced herself, but Kit didn't move. If anything, she huddled closer to herself.

"So..." Zenyth said once she was in the room, trying to make her voice as gentle as possible. "How are you doing?"

There was no response. She had a feeling that this might take a long time, so she walked over to the bed and sat down, leaving as much space as possible between her and Kit.

"Look, I'm sorry if that was rough, but I didn't know what else to do." Zenyth looked down at her hands. What had she done? Was a catatonic friend better than a brainwashed friend?

Zenyth sat quietly. Talking probably wouldn't do any good, but she wanted Kit to know that she was here for her. She had no idea how much time passed as the two of them sat there in silence. Maybe she had done more harm than good. Maybe a line had been crossed that shouldn't have been. Zenyth had wanted so desperately to make Kit realize the truth, but maybe she had gone too far.

"How many people know?"

Zenyth looked up. "What?"

Kit's head was still bowed. "About this, about me losing my mind?"

She sighed. "The rumour's spreading. A lot of theories are, honestly, quite insane, but a few are close enough that I'm wondering if someone in here said something they shouldn't have."

She wished that Kit would turn around and look at her, but she'd settle for talking.

"I want to speak to Dominika Haskell."

The statement took Zenyth by surprise. Why would Kit want to talk to the Council's liaison for Segment Delta? "I think she's back on the Centre, but we could phone and see."

"No." Kit's voice was firm. "I want to speak to her here. In person."

"It'll take at least a day to get her here from the Centre. I could bring Frederick down, if you want—"

"No. I only want to speak to Haskell."

"Would you like to get out of here and go home?" Zenyth asked gently.

There was no response. She knew better than to ask again, so she nodded to herself and stood up.

≈

"How's she doing?" Naydir asked, once Zenyth was back in the hallway.

She paused and considered her words. "It might have worked a little too well... I think she's back, but not like she used to be."

The hallway was silent as they all took in what had just happened.

Zenyth was the first to break the silence, letting out a loud sigh. "Well, I guess it's time to go to Frederick and face the consequences."

As she walked away, Naydir made a step to follow her, but Sav held him back. This had been Zenyth's idea, so they should stay out of it. This was her mess to clean up.

Zenyth was trying to be brave, but her steps were more reluctant than confident. She should have gotten Frederick's permission before doing something like this, but that would have slowed her down and she wanted to move fast. Maybe there was another solution that would have caused less damage, but time was running out.

When she reached the sixth floor, she asked Teya if Frederick was available.

"She'll be a minute or two," Teya said brightly. "You can have a seat."

Zenyth sat down and tried to keep herself under control, but every few seconds she would notice that her leg was bouncing or that her finger was tapping. She didn't usually feel anxious about things, but there was a ninety percent chance that

Frederick would yell at her. Maybe ninety-five percent.

When the door to the office opened, she stood up, but then Akola left the office and a bit more of her resolve faded away. Upon seeing Zenyth, Akola gave her the slightest of nods before exiting to the stairwell.

Zenyth took a deep breath and headed to her doom.

Sure enough, Augusta Frederick did not look impressed. She was sitting behind her desk, arms crossed, scowl on her face.

"Sit."

Zenyth obediently sat down in the chair across from the desk.

Frederick fumed for a few seconds. "You realize what you did was really stupid, right? Actually, don't answer that. You had to have known that it was stupid, because otherwise you would have run it past me."

Zenyth stayed quiet.

"You're lucky that Allen was sympathetic to your request and understands the importance of her position. She could have taken the information you gave you her and spread it all over Tecken, and who knows where that would have led? If there had been a public outcry for us to release Tyler to Tecken, then we would've had to comply. We could have lost her while she still thought she was from Tecken, and who knows what kind of revenge she would have taken on us?"

Frederick fumed again, her face red with anger. Zenyth wondered if it was possible to be banished from an island.

"Allen didn't tell me if her visit helped, so I'd appreciate knowing if your amazing plan that couldn't wait for approval actually worked, or if you've pissed me off for no reason."

Zenyth cleared her throat. "I'm pretty sure it worked."

"Pretty sure?"

"Well, Kit isn't really talking to anyone right now, but she seems sadder and more subdued."

"So you don't know for certain if it worked."

"Well..." she paused. "She told me that she wants to speak to Dominika Haskell, so that might be a good sign."

Frederick was still unimpressed. "I guess we should call Haskell right away, if that's the case."

Zenyth braced herself. "Actually, Kit wants to speak to her in person. And I don't think she's going to back down on that."

Any patience Frederick still had disappeared instantly. "Of course. Of course that's what she wants. Hansen, you're officially excused. Please get out of my face as quickly as possible."

Giving a quick respectful bow, Zenyth hurried away. If she'd realized how angry Frederick would be, then she'd have thought twice about going behind her back. She hadn't been thinking about politics, only her friend, and that may have been a mistake. Zenyth had been certain that Akola would help, but Frederick was right – this plan could have backfired spectacularly.

Naydir and Sav were waiting for her in the stairwell.

"How'd it go?" Sav asked.

"I'm alive, so better than I thought." She sighed. "Akola was leaving the office as I arrived, so Frederick already knew everything."

Naydir nodded. "So, what do we do now?"

"I don't know," she said, shrugging. "Wait for Haskell and see what happens next."

"And figure out what to tell Vaughn," Sav added.

Zenyth's heart fell into her stomach. "That's going to be another difficult one."

CHAPTER 34

Back in her own office, Akola tried not to think about what had just happened. She should have felt great for finally telling Kit off, but there was no triumph or jubilation. She'd been holding on to this anger for so long that it was impossible to let go of it in one fell swoop.

During her drive to Stanton, she'd thought about all of the possible outcomes from this visit. She could have used this opportunity to her advantage. It would've been easy to lie to Kit and say that everything was true and get the power of the Six-Elemental back on Tecken's side, but that wasn't what she wanted. Not anymore. Erikson was dead, and the island was crawling with ISS agents. There was no point in trying to make everything go back to the way it used to be, because it would never be that easy. Besides, ever since Erikson's death, Kit had been hated by most of the island's inhabitants, and Akola would never allow her to hurt these people again.

While it had been great to finally say all the things she'd been holding inside, she knew that it didn't matter. Erikson was still dead and the ISS was still in charge. Her words hadn't changed anything.

The drive back to Tecken had been fraught with emotions, but now Akola was back to her normal, controlled self. Now she had time to focus on the bigger questions, like how had something like that happened? There would likely be an investigation into this, probably headed by Stanton's ISS, but would they find anything? They didn't seem to know who had sent those letters, but it would make sense for them to suspect someone from Tecken.

She picked up the telephone and dialed a familiar number.

"Hello?"

"Pitor," she said. "How are you?"

"Quite well. And how is your day?"

"I've had better. Look, have you heard from Kendra?"

"Not recently. Why?"

"I suspect that she's been quite busy."

He paused. "Does this have anything to do with a certain rumour surrounding a certain powerful individual?"

Akola frowned, even though he couldn't see it. "I suspect so."

"Do you also suspect her of somehow being involved?"

A quick laugh escaped her lips. "Pitor, other than you, I don't know anyone else who could pull off something like that. And you'd know better than to try such a thing."

"I told her many times not to bother with the Six-Elemental, but she's gone a bit rogue ever since she decided to work for the Stanton ISS. A very Erikson thing to do, if you ask me."

"I know... Although I doubt that an Erikson would ever execute a plan so reckless." She sighed. "I had a feeling something like this might happen once she decided to work on Stanton."

"I've tried my best to guide her, but I can't push too hard or I risk losing her. When she makes up her mind, there's no changing it."

He was right. Kendra had grown up without knowing her true heritage, so she didn't have the support that an Erikson would normally have. It was all Magnus' fault, insisting that she grow up in secret because he wasn't ready to accept fatherhood yet. Akola was sure that he would've accepted Kendra later on, after he'd succeeded in taking over the Segment, but now she'd never know.

Pitor had been instrumental in giving Kendra the push she needed to get on this path. Erikson had chosen well when he appointed Pitor to watch over her, but now she was grown up, and making up her own rules. She was more like the first Magnus Erikson rather than the second, blazing her own trail through the Segment, refusing to be tied down by the past. Despite her worries, Akola couldn't help but feel proud of the woman Kendra had grown up to become.

"Well, if you happen to know anything about a certain maternal person who is inhabiting this island, it would do them well to disappear for a while."

"I don't know what you're talking about, but I'm sure it's already been taken care of. Along with the matter of another, very persuasive, individual."

"Good."

Akola ended the conversation after that. She had a feeling that Pitor knew more about this plot than he was letting on, but that wasn't necessarily a bad thing.

Besides, it was better for Pitor to lie to her. As the Leader of Tecken, Akola shouldn't know anything about any of this. She'd hidden enough of this island's skeletons after the war, and the last thing she needed was another secret to cover up.

CHAPTER 35

Once the situation had been explained, Dominika Haskell caught the next boat to Stanton. Kit still wasn't talking to anyone and refused to leave the room.

Explaining the situation to Vaughn had been as painful as Zenyth expected, especially since they couldn't confirm if Kit was back or not. The surprising part was that Vaughn didn't immediately jump to his feet and insist on seeing Kit. Zenyth didn't know if it was because he was still feeling unwell after the accident or if this time things had gone too far.

He did go with Zenyth, Naydir, and Sav to the ISS, to find out why Kit had wanted to talk to Haskell. Frederick had them wait in one of the conference rooms while the conversation took place. Nobody could think of anything to say, so they all sat around the table, silently waiting, dreading what might come next.

When Frederick finally entered the room again, she was accompanied by Haskell. The mood wasn't one of joy or happiness.

"Well," Haskell sighed, "I can confirm that Kit remembers the truth. Honestly, her brain's been worked over, but there's enough guilt in there to keep her grounded for now. Bringing in Allen was a good move. A really reckless move, and one that should have been discussed beforehand, but it did the trick."

Zenyth couldn't help feeling relieved, despite the berating. "Why did she want to talk to you?" she asked.

"She feels, and I agree with her, that it would be best for her to move to the Centre."

Zenyth's eyes widened in shock. She looked back at Vaughn, but the grim expression on his face was unchanged.

"I think it's a wise decision," Haskell continued, "considering the past couple of weeks. Nobody on this Segment will trust her anymore, I doubt she'll be able to keep her job, and if she works for the ISS people will always suspect her of being a spy. On the Centre, she'll be able to live a peaceful life. Only a few people will know who she is and where she is. We can keep her safe."

A thousand protestations rang through Zenyth's head, but she didn't say any of them. None of them mattered because Haskell was right.

"We'll be leaving tomorrow."

"So soon?" Naydir asked.

"It's best for everyone."

Zenyth preferred to disagree but remained silent.

"She wants to avoid being out in public," Frederick added, "so I'll need one of you to gather some personal items for her. Also, she mentioned that she'd like to say goodbye before she leaves. If you'd rather not talk to her, she understands, but if you'd like to see her, you can go down to the basement."

≈

Kit was sitting on the bed when Zenyth walked into the room. Zenyth could practically feel the embarrassment and shame radiating off her.

"You don't need to explain anything," Zenyth said, not giving Kit time to speak. "At least, not to me. Honestly, I expected this kind of thing to happen after the Second Invasion, so I'm only surprised that it took this long."

Kit looked up at her. There were dark circles under her eyes and her face was tight and drawn. "I shouldn't have let this happen. I should have been stronger."

Zenyth sat down next to her. "You're not a superhero, Kit. I mean, you should have told one of us what was going on, and you should have talked to someone before it got this bad. Although, having read the letters, I understand. As much as it hurts me that you thought I was a spy and not your friend, I can see how you got there. Whoever wrote those letters knew exactly what they were doing."

"It still doesn't make it right."

She rolled her eyes. "Look, if you want to beat yourself up over this, go ahead, but I won't do that to you. What's done is done, and I'm just glad to have you back in your own mind."

Kit looked at, her expression changing to a weird mix of sadness and gratitude. She leaned over and hugged Zenyth. Zenyth was taken aback, since hugging wasn't a thing they did, but she recovered quickly, putting her arms around Kit.

"You know," Zenyth said, "if this had happened a few months ago, I'd offer to go to the Centre with you, but I've got projects here that I can't abandon. Still, it doesn't mean that I won't be able to visit."

"Without you, who's going to talk sense to me?" Kit asked, breaking away from the hug.

"I guess you'll have to call me whenever you're having a crisis. I can be just as brutal over the phone."

Kit smiled, but then she looked down at her hands. "I really will miss you, Zenyth."

"I'll really miss you, too."

CHAPTER 36

When the door opened, Kit knew who it was without looking. There was only one person left for her to say goodbye to, and it was the person that she most dreaded being seeing. It had been difficult to say goodbye to Naydir and Sav, knowing that she wouldn't be able to come back for their wedding, but she knew that they'd be fine as long as they had each other. The person she was most worried about was the one standing in front of her.

Once the door was closed, Vaughn stood in front of it, not moving any further into the room. His eyes glanced her way, but were unable to stay focused on her for too long.

She wanted to go to him, to apologize, to fill the room with her remorse and regret, but there was something in his expression that made her stay where she was, sitting quietly on the bed. Before his entrance, she had been filled with guilt and shame, but the second she laid eyes on him she realized that it wasn't enough.

"You thought I was spying on you." he said quietly. "You thought that the only reason I was with you was because I was an ISS spy."

She tried to swallow the lump that was rising in her throat, but it was impossible. "The letters said—"

"I don't care what the letters said."

Kit looked down at the floor. She wanted to say that she hadn't believed the letters, but how could that be true when she'd been preparing to leave him?

"We've been together for sixteen years, Kit. Sixteen. And I know that it hasn't always been easy – but it's not for the reasons you think. You hate it when people interrupt our dates to talk to you or go to my gallery openings just to see if you'll be there, but none of that bothered me. Even the dreams about Nathan weren't enough to ever make me want to leave." He took a deep breath and tried to steady himself. "What really troubled me was that you always had one foot out the door. Not in the beginning, when you were determined to make things work, but afterwards. It felt like you were holding me at arm's length. I didn't need you to marry me to prove a point – marriage doesn't matter that much to me – but we never so much as talked about the possibility. Whenever the topic came up, you'd freeze, and I'd know what it meant."

"Vaughn..." her voice caught in her throat.

"All I wanted from you was a reaction that wasn't blind panic. I deserved better than that."

It felt as if someone had reached inside her chest and was crushing her heart. Everything he'd said was true. She'd been so worried that he was going to leave her that she never truly committed to him. She was so convinced that she would ruin everything, and in the end she'd done exactly that.

"You deserve better than me," she said, her voice cracking with emotion. "It was easy for me to think that you were a spy, because I couldn't understand why you were still with me when I was such a burden. When you were in the hospital, I couldn't visit you because I was too messed up to put your needs ahead of my own, but if the situation had been reversed, you would have been at my side day and night, spy or not. It's not fair to you."

"So, you're giving up?" he said flatly.

"I can't ask you to forgive me. What I did was horrible."

"But do you want me to forgive you? Or are you done?"

His expression was difficult to read, and she wasn't sure how to respond. Every time she thought about saying goodbye to him, she could feel a tightness in her chest.

"What about the next time, Vaughn? Or the time after that? Because, knowing me, there will always be a next time. You should be with someone who won't keep hurting you the way that I do – the way that I can't seem to stop hurting you."

Vaughn leaned back against the door and put his head in his hands. "Listen, I know that I could have walked away any time I wanted, so don't make me out to be some kind of hopeless romantic with no backbone."

"I didn't—"

"I made mistakes, too. I know what it looks like when something's bothering you, when you're about to spiral into one of your episodes, but I was too afraid to do anything. I thought that if I pushed you to talk to someone about it, you'd leave me, so I did nothing. I'll never know if I could have helped you avoid all this, but I know that I can't go back to the way things were." He sighed and shook his head. "But I'm not ready to give up."

It felt as if the world had slowed down. "What?" Kit said, her mouth dropping open

He looked up, and when his eyes locked with hers, Kit realized that he was serious.

"I can't stay here," she said.

"Then I'll go with you."

The thought of Vaughn accompanying her to the Centre

was like a light in the darkness. The idea that he might want to come with her had never crossed her mind, but now it was all she could think about.

But it wouldn't be fair. She couldn't let him leave everything behind to be exiled with her. It would be a terrible thing to ask of him, and she was tired of being selfish.

"No," she said, trying to sound strong. "I can't let you follow me to the Centre. It wouldn't be right."

"I wouldn't be following you, I'd be going with you. Besides," and the barest hint of a smile appeared on his face, "it's not like I have a studio here anymore."

Despite his attempt at humour, she didn't feel better. "Vaughn, I don't want you offering to go with me because of pity or some noble sense of honour."

He let out a frustrated cry. "You really don't get it, do you? Kit, I love you. I'm really, really upset with you right now, but I still love you. And I'm not upset that someone got into your head and preyed on your weaknesses, I'm frustrated that you never talked to anyone about it. People have been trying to help you since the Second Invasion, but you've been too stubborn to let them."

She hated that he was right.

"I'm willing to work on this relationship and see if we can save it, but I refuse to do it alone. If I go with you to the Centre, it has to be because you love me and want me there, and you're determined to make this work. Because if I go with you and you keep heading down the same path you're on now, I won't hesitate to leave. So, if you don't want to put in the time or effort, then we might as well say goodbye right now."

A million thoughts waged war inside her head. The past indicated that no matter what she did, she would fail and the relationship would fall apart. It would be easier to break up now and stop holding on. But, if there was a chance that she could save this, shouldn't she take it? The one thing she knew for certain was that she never wanted to feel this hopeless ever again. She needed to change – needed to be a better person. And if it meant that she could keep Vaughn in her life, then she had to try.

For the first time in days she felt hope for the future.

Vaughn took her silence as resignation and started to move for the door.

"Wait!" she cried out, stepping forward. "I'll try. I can't guarantee that I'll do everything perfectly, but I'll try. I promise. For you, I'll do anything."

CHAPTER 37

When Frederick informed her that the Six-Elemental had been relocated off the Segment, Akola couldn't help feeling relieved. Now that Kit was gone, hopefully the memory of everything that had happened between the two of them would stop haunting her and she'd be able to move past her anger.

Initially, Frederick had called to provide an update on the Briton Investigation. The Stanton ISS was crafting a plan and would be putting out a notice for volunteers soon. If Akola had any employees from the ISS or Tecken Police that she trusted, then she was welcome to submit them, but the final decisions would be made by Frederick's team, based on skills and compatibility. Akola said that she would look for appropriate people but knew that it was very unlikely anyone from Tecken would be chosen. At least she would receive updates on the investigation, no matter who was selected.

Although Stanton's ISS was taking all the credit for this investigation, Akola knew who the real mastermind was. It was no coincidence that something like this was happening mere months after Kendra started working for them. Taking on Briton was a smart move, not just for her career, but also as a step to becoming a beloved Leader. Now that the Six-Elemental was no longer an obstacle, Akola had no doubt that Kendra would rise even higher.

Frederick mentioned that the ISS was no closer to figuring out who had sent the letters to Kit, or who the person posing as her mother had been, or where Wes was located, but they were still searching any leads that came up. There was a general suspicion that Kit had imagined the meeting with her mother, which Akola was relieved to hear. Kit's mental state had been questionable towards the end, and it helped that when the ISS came to investigate, there had been no yellow house with a blue door on that street. As underhanded as it was, she had to respect Pitor's thoroughness and speed.

Although Akola still thought that the plan had been reckless, she was able to admire what Kendra had achieved. She'd managed to ruin the Six-Elemental's reputation throughout the entire Segment. Nobody would ever think of her as a hero again – she would merely be a flawed Elemental who had outlived her usefulness. Akola wondered if it had always been a part of the plan to cause Kit to leave the Segment or if it was a welcome side-effect. Whatever the case, it was a spectacular effort – one that would have made Kendra's biological father proud.

Akola had always hoped that Kendra would pick up where Magnus had left off, to lead the people of Tecken with that same drive and determination that he'd had. Although Kendra was currently forging her own path, Akola couldn't help wondering if it would be better than anything Pitor and she could have imagined. Maybe this time an Erikson would finally succeed.

Although she hadn't been around for most of Kendra's life, it was amazing to watch her living up to her true potential. Akola couldn't help feeling a wash of pride as her biological daughter stepped into the shoes of her father, proving herself to be a true Erikson.

CHAPTER 38

As Kit watched Segment Delta grow more distant, she finally felt the full sense of what she'd lost. Never again would she set foot on these islands. She had no idea what life on the Centre would be like, but hopefully she would be able to make it her home. She'd done it before – after her father's death, when Briton became a jail, she'd made Stanton her home. Her only hope was that she wouldn't mess up again, because eventually she'd run out of places to live.

One small comfort was the picture that Vaughn had brought. When he'd arrived at the dock with his bag packed, he had also been carrying the picture of the streetlamp that she'd admired at the gallery opening. The exhibit had closed a few days ago, so its arrival was just in time. Looking at the picture reminded her of how perfect that night had been, and how even though she was in darkness right now, there was still light.

Vaughn was currently below deck, lying down in one of the cabins. Things were still strained between then, so she was spending most of her time on deck, watching the water. It had been difficult getting used to the boat and the motion of the waves, and within the first thirty minutes she almost asked them to take her back, but eventually she adapted. This trip would last at least half a day, depending on the weather, which would hopefully be favourable. If the motor broke down, she'd gladly offer to push the boat with her powers. Maybe she should have offered anyway.

Truthfully, this was long overdue. She should have left the Segment years ago, after she'd finished cleaning up the mess that she was responsible for, but instead she'd been selfish. All she'd ever wanted was to be normal, but the truth was that she was anything but, and it was unfair for her to expect anyone else to think that she was. She'd resented the Followers of Six for thinking she was a god, when their religion had been around a lot longer than she had. She'd resented anyone who glared at her or said hateful things because it reminded her of all the terrible things she'd done and made her wonder if her actions had truly helped anyone.

She'd been living with these regrets and fears for so long, but had been too scared to do anything about it. Instead of accepting that her life had changed and she should change with it, she'd ignored all the signs. But ignoring problems didn't solve them. Problems didn't come with expiry dates.

It would have been better if she hadn't ruined her entire reputation beforehand, but maybe that was her punishment for not going away sooner.

Her life would never be normal. The best she could hope for was some kind of peace.

EPILOGUE

"Apparently Stanton is now Six-Elemental-free."

Kendra looked over to see Skye standing in the bedroom doorway, holding a newspaper. "Apparently?" she said, turning back to the mirror and giving her outfit one final glance.

Skye smirked and rolled her eyes. "You'd know more than I would, ISS employee." She stepped into the room and handed Kendra the *Stanton News*, pointing at the article she'd just read.

Quickly glancing over the article, Kendra read how the reporter had watched Kit Tyler get on a boat with her partner and Dominika Haskell yesterday, heading off to parts unknown. They speculated that Tyler was heading to The Centre, but acknowledged that she could be heading to any other Segment. The reporter had contacted the ISS for further comment on the matter, but the ISS was staying silent.

"Think you'll be able to get the story at work today?" Skye asked.

"I'm still not able to get a straight answer to whether or not she went crazy, but if I hear anything, I'll let you know," she smiled.

"You're the best spy ever," Skye said, wrapping her arms around Kendra. "Well, maybe not ever, but at least you try."

Kendra couldn't help laughing. "Thank you for the confidence boost." She gave Skye a quick kiss. "Are we still on for the movie tonight?"

"Only if you don't have some juicy gossip to discuss."

She laughed again. "I'll see you after work. Have a good day."

"You too."

Skye's apartment wasn't as close to the ISS building as Kendra's was, but Kendra didn't mind the longer walk to work – especially today. Pitor had already informed her that Tyler was no longer in Segment Delta, but the news report was just the confirmation she needed. The report showed no sadness or regret about Tyler's leaving, or any attempt to hide or discredit the rumours that had been swirling around the past couple of weeks.

Kendra couldn't help smiling. It was beneficial for a leader to eliminate every threat in her way instead of hoping that they wouldn't affect her, and she had done just that with the Six-Elemental. Not only had she ruined Tyler's reputation, but Tyler would have to think long and hard before showing her face in Segment Delta again.

Her thoughts turned to the Briton Investigation, and how well it was coming along. Their plan was to place a few obvious plants within the police, along with a number of spies who would be able to infiltrate the Humanists and get to the truth. It was only a matter of time before they had enough people in place to see what was really going on in Briton.

Once the truth about the Humanists' deception came out, it'd be easier for her to achieve her true goal – creating a united governing body over the entire Segment. After all, how could they continue to maintain peace and avoid another war if each island was busy obeying its own rules? Each Leader needed to be held accountable to the others, and it'd be easier to do that if there was one person overseeing everyone.

There was still a long way to go, but she'd get there eventually. Pitor might have wanted her to become Kendra Erikson, the Fifth Queen of Tecken, but she had other plans. Bigger plans. If all went well, one day, she would be the First Queen of Segment Delta.

It was only a matter of time.

The early years of **Xander Drew** as he struggles with the evils of his small rural hometown of Coral Beach, Maine. Cursed with the heart of the Womb and the gift of seeing the world around him for what it really is, Xander must learn the hard lessons about the nature of humanity to traverse the minefield of criminals, gangs, and abusers that stand between him and ultimate happiness -- but most of all that **sometimes it takes a monster, to catch a monster.**

The Coral Beach Casefiles series by Matthew LeDrew:

For more information, please visit

www.engenbooks.com

ABOUT THE AUTHOR

Alison House is an Award-Winning, Best-selling author, a playwright, a traveler, and a reader.

A native Newfoundlander, House is a graduate of the Fine Arts program at Sir Wilfred Grenfell College (MUN). She currently resides in Halifax, Nova Scotia, where she works in arts administration and spends more time than a person should in and around theaters.

House won the December 2018 Kit Sora Prize, which celebrates authors throughout Canada. Her short fiction has appeared in every issue of the *From the Rock* anthology series, as well as *Bluenose Paradox* and the *Kit Sora Artobiography*.

The Fifth Queen is her second novel.